CASH

Keepers

A "Dope-Tale"
By:
D'Shon Major

Platform Bookhouse Publishing

P.O Box 252

Del Valle, Tx 78617

Printed in the United States of America

Published by:

Platform Bookhouse Publishing

ISBN : 979-8-9944488-2-3

Library of Congress Control Number: 2026910592

Email: platformbookhousepublishing@gmail.com

Website: pbhpublishing.com

Check us out on our social media platforms:

TikTok: @pbptok02

Facebook: Platform Bookhouse Publishing

Instagram: Platform Bookhouse Publishing

Author's Note

What Is a Cash Keeper?

A lot of people think they understand what a Cash Keeper is… or isn't. They hear Cash Keeper and immediately think of money—the hustle, the shine, the glory—but not the story. But if that's all you see, then you're missing the bigger picture. A Cash Keeper ain't just somebody getting money or stacking it. It's somebody who levels up and understands everything that comes with it. Because money brings power—but it also brings problems. Problems that show up at your doorstep with choices that don't always come with clean morals attached. And once you step into that world, everything around you starts revealing itself for what it really is… not what you thought it was. A Cash Keeper stands in the middle of that chaos—and holds it together. So as you flip these pages, pay attention to the decisions. The risks. The moments where everything could've gone sideways—and sometimes did. That's what this life is about. Not just chasing a bag… but living with whatever it costs to keep it. Because at the end of the day—Cash keeping ain't just a hustle. It's a way of life.

-D'Shon Major
Platform Bookhouse Publishing
Home of the Streets

Dedication

This book is dedicated to the hustlers (Cash Keepers) who learned survival before they learned peace. To those who keep going when quitting is easier. This is for you.

Introduction

Once Pop tasted freedom after doing a 5-year prison bid. He came home hungrier than before and jumped back on the hustle like he had never left. His jailhouse vacation had done the opposite of slowing him down. It sharpened his mentality for putting together twos and fews, and fueled his ghetto dreams of hood stardom. The second he hit the free ground, nothing was about to stop him from getting filthy rich.

Even locked up, the hustle never stopped. Instead of snow white and straight drop, Pop stacked money behind bars, pushing packs of loose tobacco and pounds of Reggie. He ran free-world plays from inside, and bribed prison officials into doing the most. Whatever he wanted slid through them gates, nearly tripling in price once hitting the cell block.

He walked out the cage with grind money on his books and the number to a Colombian plug he met on the inside, both tucked away like weapons. His only regret? Leaving his baby mama, Remy, and most of all, his son — Foreal Jr. — to hold it down while he served time.

While Pop was locked up paying street dues, Mom made sure Foreal still had ties to his daddy's side. Most weekends, she dropped him at Maw-Maw's spot — Pop's mother — deep in East Austin. The part of town where the blocks were hot, the corners stayed lit, and the air smelled like dirty money and gunpowder.

Foreal's uncles, Ricky and Bo, were strung high on getting money and played the game for keeps. While one side of Foreal's family preached about education and hard work, Pop's side originated hustlers and lawbreakers of all sorts. Before Pop took a fall, he and his brothers had carved out a name for themselves inside the Booker T. Washington projects — better known as the Bricks.

Maw-Maw's house was just a block away from the hangout, so it didn't take long before the hood became Foreal's second home. He was already late-night hanging, and getting used to the rhythm of the streets. For Foreal, walking in Pop's shadow was unshakable, and soaking up the game came naturally.

Riding the Capitol Metro bus became routine when school let out on Fridays. It was Foreal's way of sliding to the East Side, and linking up with the boys from the projects. On the day of seeing Pop again, that's exactly where he was found.

$ $ $ $ $

Pop pulled up flossing in a '94 Buick Roadmaster sitting pretty on 23-inch Lionhearts. The trunk pounded so heavy it shook the block, bass rattling like it was ready to crack concrete. You couldn't stand next to it with a drink in your hand without spilling. Rapper T.I. blasted from the speakers when Foreal hopped in, and just like that, father and son were back in motion.

At first, Foreal fought the urge of asking Pop to turn the music down. The bass slapped so hard it rattled his skull. But he knew better than to look soft. Instead, he leaned back, rocked his head, and took the full punishment of the woofers.

Like old times, Pop wasted no time rolling around and showing his boy off. He slid him through the Highland Mall, straight to Foot Locker, and copped him a fresh pair of red-and-white Jordan 11s. Yeah, Pop was back.

That Friday, Foreal took the city bus out to Pop's crib, strolling up just as the pizza man did. He knocked on the door and was met by a thick, caramel-brown beauty, no older than twenty-five. She wore a black-and-red halter top, skin-tight capris, and matching retro 10s. She was a grown woman, and fine, the type that made you forget what you came for.

"What's up, lil' nigga?" she asked, sizing him up, one hand on her hip.

Foreal almost choked on his candy, but his voice came out steady. "What's up?" The bass in his fifteen-year-old pipes barely held, but it was enough.

The girl grabbed the pizzas, bounced back inside, and yelled, "Ko, yo son here!" Her ass jiggled as she disappeared, leaving Foreal standing there half-shook.

Everybody called Pop "Ko-Baby." Why? Foreal had no idea. It didn't matter. He followed the fine chick to the back where Pop lounged in a thick cloud of smoke. The room reeked of kush the second Foreal stepped in.

"Nika, put that shit out! Damn!" Pop barked, irritated at having to raise his voice.

Nika smacked her lips but obeyed. She stubbed the blunt out in a marble ashtray, her eyes still locked on Pop. Out the blue and without warning, Nika blurted out, "Shid, that lil' nigga probably blow anyway."

Foreal's eyes shot to hers, only to find her staring right back.

"Yeah, nigga. I know," she said, like it was already written.

Foreal dipped his head shyly, gazing at the floor before grabbing two pizza slices to take with him. Pop shook his head but Nika had already taken a liking to him. From that day on, their bond grew fast.

She showered him with attention and showed love like he was her own little brother. Told him straight up how much he reminded her of Pop —

not just in his face but in his vibe. Since she trusted Pop heavy, she stretched that same energy toward Foreal without hesitation.

Soon she was sliding him money, taking him shopping, and making sure he stayed fresh when the school year popped. Nika moved slick. She even slipped him sticky to smoke on the low, warning him not to tell Pop. But snitching wasn't in Foreal's bloodline.

Nika was the female version of Pop in every way. A hard hustler, sharp with her tongue, and all-the-way street. She was bossy, sassy, and deadly rolled into one. On top of that, she had a mean squabble and Foreal saw firsthand how she handled hers when a chick tried to test her. Nika left no doubts — she wasn't to be played with.

To Foreal, she was everything a true hustler could ask for in a woman. A rider. A soldier. Somebody who matched Pop's energy bar for bar.

As Foreal edged closer to sixteen, he prayed that when the game called for him to lace his own boots, he'd have his mind locked on cash and a down chick like Nika at his side — just like Pop

One

Foreal had the feel good jitters when he celebrated his sixteenth birthday. Nika turned out to be an expert party planner, pulling together a teenagers-only buzz that had the whole hood lit. Flyers hit the poles, word spread fast, and before long everybody knew the party was the place to be.

By now, Foreal had earned his nickname — *Young Ham*. Nika stayed clowning, calling him that around family and friends until it stuck. When his birthday finally rolled around, the celebration lived up to the hype. His closest homies were all present, and the Eastside came deep.

The house was packed wall-to-wall with bodies moving in rhythm to bass-heavy beats. Sweat dripped off foreheads, the air was thick with cologne, perfume, and the faint smell of liquor and smoke. Laughter and screams intertwined with the music, a chaos that somehow made sense. Pop locked Max, his mean-as-hell Doberman, in the back room to keep the party alive.

As the energy spilled outside, Young Ham leaned against the wall, watching the scene, but his mind wasn't on them. He kept scanning the crowd, lowkey wondering if that one shorty from school was really pulling up.

Around ten, his question was answered. Kamiko strolled in like she owned the air she breathed. She didn't even try to blend in. She found a spot by herself near the patio door, and swayed to the music, finding her groove.

Kamiko had that light-skinned glow from her Puerto Rican pops, mixed with her Black mother's curves straight from the motherland. Long, curly hair flowed down her back like a waterfall. Their eyes locked, and Young Ham made his move, practicing what to say under his breath. Her blush gave him the green light — she was feeling him.

Yeah, she had a boyfriend, but Young Ham wasn't worried. In his mind, she'd be his arm candy soon enough.

"Happy birthday, Young Ham," Kamiko said as he approached.

"Thanks, babygirl," he replied, pulling her into a hug. His hands slid low, grabbing at her curves.

"Boy, don't get slapped on your birthday," she teased, pushing him back with a smile.

"My bad. Thought you was my gift."

"Keep playin', I'ma punch you," she laughed. "Your party is really something. Glad I came."

"Me too," Young Ham said, leaning in closer. "I was 'bout to put an APB out if you didn't show."

They both laughed, the music pounding so loud it forced Young Ham to tilt his head, lips close to her ear as he kept the conversation player-like. The chemistry was there and everyone else faded into background noise.

They stayed glued together the rest of the night, talking low, and brushing against each other. Pop tapped Young Ham's shoulder to shut it down. Past one in the morning, the party was fading, and folks were calling rides and dipping out.

Just when Young Ham thought Kamiko was loosening up, her phone buzzed in her pocket. She pulled away, answering a call from her mom outside. Young Ham tried to hold her close, leaning in for a kiss, but Kamiko dodged and let it land on her cheek.

Kamiko stepped back toward the patio door, eyes sharp but teasing. "Young Ham, you know I got a boyfriend. Bye."

She tossed a smile over her shoulder as she disappeared into the night.

Young Ham stood there smiling, shaking his head. "Yeah, I know... but that chump out of there."

Two

Mom's house had become less of Young Ham's bed and board. Between Pop's spot and Maw-Maw's house, that's where he lay his head most nights. A big part of that came from school expelling him over a fight that wasn't even his fault.

Some fool wanted an audience and showed off in front of the cafeteria crowd. He stepped to Young Ham wrong, and paid the price. Unfortunately, the show-off caught the worst of it, getting busted up and embarrassed all at once. Young Ham found out later the scuffle had traces of being gang-related. The set tripper pushed play on Young Ham, who was caught walking the hallways rocking a Kansas City Chiefs tee and a matching red-and-yellow fitted.

Gangbanging and color boundaries had swept through the city like a plague, but Young Ham barely cared. Eastside OGs like B. Russ and Pick introduced zip codes as a rep badge for claiming turf through numbers such as: 78721, -24, -41, -53, and of course, 02 — that was Young Ham's district.

$ $ $ $ $

Pop and his brothers combined their money and opened up a shop on Airport Blvd — Rolling Thunder. Upholstery, paint, and mechanics all under one roof. The oldest, Bo, ran the joint. He drove a '95 Chevy Impala with enough bang in the trunk to rattle teeth. If you dared ride in the backseat too long. Uncle Bo was the go-to when you wanted your whip detailed and pounding.

Young Ham caught on quickly. Nowadays when he hassled Pop for a few extras, he got the "money-don't-grow-on-trees" speech, and when Pop called him into the shop, he always left pocketing a hundred or more. His clothes stayed stained in soap from washing cars, grease from moving tires — but the work came with perks. Whatever was left behind in the cars became his. Most days, he and the homies hung around Rolling Thunder just to check the scene.

Rolling Thunder was the spot where better than average hustlers earned stripes. "Big money takes little money," dice games ran hot on the boulevard. Original bone-shakers like Big Tre from 12th Street and Gambler from the Hogpin came through shooting big. Loud music blasted, bankrolls flashed, and playboys stalked the ladies.

When the dice game circled up, money flooded the pavement. Lil Head Ced spat: "Y'all niggas ain't eatin' like two-one Shack Texas. I'm shootin' a Benjamin every time I touch the dice." He tossed his backpack full of knots like proof.

Crooked L from Mason Manor clapped back. "Yeah, I'm fading that big six talk. In case you forgot, Red Brick Clique money like the 'lac I drive… old and long."

Turbo, Saint John's finest, jumped in wild. "After I break you niggas, I'ma buy that red 'lac parked outside and spray it candy blue next week. Now tee-lee niggas."

Pop, cool as always, leaned in with his bankroll, face unreadable. He stayed quiet while others boasted. He didn't need words. His money spoke loud enough. If challenged, he simply laid his bills down and said, "Bet, hustler."

Young Ham watched and learned. He studied the dice games, the hustlers, the crews. 44 Dove Springs boys from the Southside flaunted diamond bird chains with ruby-red eyes — signs of their clique.

"One of you ballers loan me ten stacks till my disability check come in," 23-AL from Bundyhill shouted, clowning. He hollered at Pop from time to time, and always left the house carrying a suitcase. Guess he took frequent trips. Who knows?

The stacks of money exchanging fists made Young Ham inventory his own pockets. Empty. Here he was, the son of a hustler — yet sitting broke. The shame stung.

Stealing bikes and running petty licks had run its course. It wasn't cutting it. Young Ham promised himself the moment had come. No more childish games. It was time to dip his toes deeper, and get paid.

Two hours later, the dice game wrapped up. Pop, Crooked L, and one other stuffed dirty bills in their jeans, sweat dripping. Young Ham asked Pop how much he won. Pop tossed him two rough-looking C-notes, then broke off a fat face apiece to Young Ham's homies. They thanked him and walked back toward the hood.

Young Ham's mind spun on the walk back. He needed to get his hands on real money. Not pocket change. Not handouts. Real street paper. The kind that punched haters in the gut. One thing about Young Ham, once he made his mind up, it was final.

He wasn't one nor two feet in the game but could speak the language; work, juice, hard, ya-yo. Or whatever else a dealer came with on a whim. Some of his partners had left the porch early, and were already eating like hogs on the blocks. His biggest issue? He didn't know how to serve a pinch of dope without giving it away like government cheese.

Everyday he encountered crack buyers like it was the normal thing.

That was easy. Smokers stalked the hood daily, looking to get right. Most geeked out of habit, and asked outright, "Youngster, you got some work?"

As he and his crew walked down Harvey Street, another thought burned his mind. Pop had ties to nearly every hustle in the city. How could he move without getting exposed? If Pop found out, it'd cripple his grind before it even had a chance to grow.

"You all quiet, my nigga. What's up?" *Youngin'* asked. He was the youngest in the crew, but looked at Young Ham like a big brother, even though only two years split them.

"I'm thinkin'," Young Ham said, eyes hard. "Thinkin' how these other niggas out here gettin' money… and we stuck in last place."

The crew fell silent. He knew they were with him on this, and they understood he wasn't talking just to hear himself. Young Ham finally spoke. "It's time to stop playin'. The hood depends on it."

Pop always said, "A man without a plan is only half a man with one." Young Ham had a plan and it started with Stacks, a day-one homie who was already caught in the mix.

Young Ham and Stacks first bumped heads on the same little league baseball team, the Sharks. Both wanted the starting pitcher job, and that drove a wedge between them. After one ugly Saturday loss, they fought over who was to blame.

Fists flew behind the coach's house, two hard rounds before the 210-pound coach stormed out, yelling at them to run laps. Young Ham and Stacks looked at him like he was crazy, then laughed and blasted off.

"Run yo Fat Albert ass some laps — we quit!"

They squashed the beef and walked home together. That was the last ball they ever pitched, but the first bond they ever formed. Stacks stayed in the Bricks with his T-Jones and little brother. Young Ham was a block away with his grandma on Goodwin Ave.

"Man, I ain't gon' lie," Stacks said, "I thought only wetbacks stayed on that street."

From that moment on, they were locked in tight.

Three

Fat Mack was a prolific hustler from around the way, holding OG status when it came to bust-downs and sticky green. Big as he was, the city crowned him "The Pimp"—not for the women he had, but because of the sharp dress code and the kind of drawl that made him sound like Biggie himself.

Stacks had already hit Fat Mack, letting him know they'd be posted at the top of the hill by the office building. About thirty minutes later, Fat Mack rolled up in his old-school trophy; glass-house rims glistening, vogues hugging the curb. He crept into the lot at a snail's pace, music rattling so hard the walls shook.

After Youngin' ducked out quick from catching bubble guts, Young Ham and Stacks found themselves a random porch to post up on. That was the hood's routine—everyone borrowed a porch at some point in the day. If somebody got upset inside and told them to move, they'd clap back with the same line every time.

"This ain't your porch, this government property!"

Everyone would fall out laughing, because it was the truth.

Young Ham, though, stayed quiet. Head down, eyes locked on the ground while Fat Mack left the car running and stepped out. Stacks and Fat Mack handled business, and Young Ham tried to blend into the background like he was invisible. He figured if he kept still, maybe nobody would notice him.

But soon as Fat Mack finished up, he glanced over and said, "Ssssup, Young Ham? What chu doin'?"

"Huh?" Young Ham stuttered, caught off guard. "Oh, nothin'."

Fat Mack squinted at him, shook his head, then hopped back in the Oldsmobile. Soon as Fat Mack pulled off, Stacks pounced.

"Damn, my nigga. You stiff as a statue. Thought you was the Statue of Liberty the way you standin'!"

Stacks kept firing jokes, laughing so hard he wiped tears from his eyes. "Bro, you looked constipated, like you was 'bout to pass out."

When he finally caught his breath, he dug into his pocket and handed Young Ham a quarter-ounce of crack.

Until that day, Young Ham had never touched crack. But now, holding it in his palm, it felt like destiny itself. The weight of it carried power. His chest burned and determination dwelled in his eyes. *I'ma be that nigga they love to hate.*

Stacks noticed the fire in Young Ham's eyes and grinned. "I believe you, my nigga. But first, we gotta hit the store and grab a razor so we can bust this down right."

He led the way downhill toward Big Al's, cracking small talk, but Young Ham barely heard him. He was locked in his own head, thinking about Mom. The guilt hit him—knowing she'd be torn apart if she found out he carried the same heart Pop had. The heart of a hustler.

Four

Stacks pounded his fists against the screen door of Apartment 1301. Clang… clang… clang…. The noise echoed through the projects, waking up half the block. Young Ham shifted nervously, clutching the dope in his pocket, eyes darting around to see if anybody was watching. Unlike Stacks, who was cool and at ease, Young Ham felt the bad omen of standing too long in one spot with work on him.

"Who is this?" a raspy voice yelled from inside.

"Its me, Stacks," he replied. The sound of locks twisting and chains jingling followed, then the door swung open with surprising energy. Young Ham tensed up.

"Y'all ain't about to stand on my porch all day drawin' heat. Come on in," the woman snapped.

Inside, the apartment was dim, sheets covering the windows letting only slivers of light through. Young Ham felt the stale air, expecting the sour stench of a smoker's den, but instead the place smelled faintly clean— better than expected.

"Jamal, who this you bringing up in my house?" the woman demanded.

"Liana, I told you my name Stacks. And this my nigga, Young Ham," Stacks said coolly.

"Boy, your name Jamal. Joyce didn't name you no damn Stacks," Liana shot back. "Keep playin', I'ma ask her myself."

Stacks threw up his hands in surrender. "A'ight, Liana, you win. But me and my pat'na need to chop this work real quick."

Liana rolled her eyes, then went upstairs. "Y'all better leave me something. And Jamal—you still owe me from last time," she called down.

Stacks and Young Ham ducked into the kitchen, sitting at a rickety wooden table that looked ready to collapse. Young Ham leaned on it lightly while Stacks unwrapped the package.

"Look, I'ma do this before my baby pull up. Pay attention, homie," Stacks said, pulling out the razor Young Ham had just bought. He engraved the pre-cook down the middle, snapping off a chunk that resembled a french fry. With quick motions, he broke it into five pinky-nail size stones.

"These go for twenty apiece. Non-negotiable." He slid the dope and razor back to Young Ham. "It's on you now."

Young Ham copied the moves, and broke down the rest. By the time he was finished, he had fifteen hustlers' stones next to the five Stacks already cut.

"Damn, nigga, you wasn't playin'," Stacks said, giving props. "You did that shit like a pro—barely got crumbs. You might be built for this."

When Liana came back down, Young Ham was tucking the last rock inside a used baggie leftover from an earlier blunt.

"Come on, Jamal. Give me something," she demanded, one hand on her hip, palm outstretched.

Young Ham dropped two stones in her hand without hesitation. Her eyes nearly popped out at the bright yellow cubes.

"Thank you for yo hospitality," he said with a smirk.

"I like him already," Liana grinned. "Knows how to give back to the game."

Before they could say more, a heavy-handed knock rattled the door. Liana popped her juice under her tongue and moved quickly to answer. Young Ham's heart pounded. He hadn't been in the game for ten minutes and was already picturing cops rushing in.

Liana cracked the door and slid her slim frame in the gap. "What you want, Greg?" She opened the door fully, closing and locking up once the dusty white man passed.

"What you want, Greg?" she asked again.

"Mmph… thirty dollars' worth," Greg muttered.

Stacks nudged Young Ham. "Nigga, hit the lick."

"Oh yeah," Young Ham fumbled inside the crack sack ignorantly. He looked up at Stacks for guidance and got nothing.

"Hood, you greener than that dank we blew. Don't forget each rock a dub. Be out here having a half-off sale while I'm gone," Stacks said, clowning Young Ham's on-the-job training.

Young Ham hurried to bust a twenty in half, finally getting it right and handing it over. Greg inspected the goods, grinned a toothless smile, then dropped two dirty bills in Young Ham's palm.

That was it. Young Ham had recorded and sold his first rocks in the dope game. Official now. If dollars came this easy, he'd get rich in no time, or so he thought.

Liana and Greg went upstairs to get high, leaving Young Ham soaking in what just happened. He'd only been in the game an hour and was moving product at a breeze. The rush of it had his chest tight with adrenaline.

Stacks lifted his phone and peered at the screen. "Fam, my bitch outside. I'ma fuck with you later." He walked toward the stairs and hollered up. "Liana, I'm bouncing, come lock up."

Young Ham and Stacks stepped off the porch, embracing in a G-hug and slapping palms twice—their ritual.

"No matter what we call it, this shit ain't no game," Stacks said, his tone sharp. "Shit can get fucked up real fast. Don't get drunk off that sweet taste, you feel me?"

Young Ham nodded, taking it in.

Stacks climbed into a Jolly Rancher grape -colored Cadillac Fleetwood that gleamed with gold trim and Daytonas. A chandelier swung from the ceiling inside, giving the car a showroom glow. Its driver was Princess—thirty-two, chocolate-skin, a mouth full of gold teeth, and leader of the infamous Gamine Girls. They were known for rolling deep in candy-painted 'Lacs and putting young hustlers on game.

As the Caddy pulled off, Young Ham caught the lesson. The streets had rules, ups and downs, and wages to pay. He wasn't blind to none.

Back inside, Liana leaned against the doorway. "Young Ham, you can post up here if you want. Safer than standing on the block."

That didn't sound half bad. "That's a bet, Liana."

By 6:35 p.m., Young Ham was set up in her living room, the dull-colored sofa pushed against the wall, a chipped coffee table holding up a crooked lamp with no shade. He sat in the kitchen instead, keeping his eyes on the door.

"Answer if somebody knock," Liana called from upstairs.

Sure enough, a faint tap came at the front screen. Young Ham slid over to the window, peeking through. A thin woman stood outside in a knitted sweater despite the heat. She raised a shaky hand and flashed a wrinkled $20 bill.

Young Ham opened the door, wondering what she had going on waving dirty money in the open. She slid inside without a word. Deaf. She pointed to her pocket. Young Ham dropped the work in her pouch, and she headed upstairs. Smooth exchange.

As the night rolled on, customers came steady. Every ten minutes, a knock. Young Ham stayed sharp, pushing ten dollars or better each time. No discounts, no handouts. Either you hustled up more greenbacks, or did business elsewhere.

An hour later, Liana came back down, fresh from a shower. Her hair was damp and hung past her shoulders, showing its true length. She wore an oversized Mickey Mouse tee and pajama pants.

"You got more work, Young Ham?" she asked.

"Yeah. One rock left. What it do?" He was ready to call it a night.

Liana stepped closer, voice low. "I don't got no money, Young Ham. But let me work for it."

Young Ham froze, her words catching him off guard. "Nigga," she said, looking dead in his eyes. "Let me give you some head for that last stone. Know you ain't had no pussy" She wasn't wrong. Young Ham's chest pounded as he looked her up and down. She seemed clean, and had all her teeth. Without another thought, Liana dropped to her knees, sliding his shorts down on the way. Her warm mouth worked magic until the last rock was hers. He left Liana's apartment tickled and light-headed, and $340 richer. He staggered inside Maw-Maw's crib, and laid it down for the night, feeling like a new man. From this day forward, he knew nothing would ever be the same. Lying in bed, he pictured flipping apartment 1301 into his own version of "New Jack City's," Carter.

Five

The smell of Maw-Maw's cooking pulled Young Ham out of a deep dream—one where he stood on top of the world clutching a fist full of dollars. Sleepy-eyed, he drifted into the kitchen and planted a kiss on the pretty old woman's cheek.

"Good morning, pretty lady," he said, grabbing his plate off the counter.

After gobbling two pancakes, eggs, and bacon, he hit the shower. By the time he came out, somebody banged heavy on the front door.

"I got it, Maw-Maw," he hollered, finishing up in the back before she could even move. Pop stood at the door when he opened it.

He hurried to throw on some white Dickie shorts, a black tee with "*I got work!* "printed across the chest, and slid into all black Air Max 95s. He stepped into the den just as Pop finished eating.

"What's up, Pop?"

"Let's roll." Pop didn't bother asking what Young Ham had planned. He stood up, walked out the door, and didn't wait for a reply.

"Come lock the screen, Maw-Maw! I'll be back later," Young Ham called out, hopping into the passenger seat of a brand-new Dodge Ram 1500.

"Hey, what's good, Pop?" Young Ham tried again, still sensing the weight on his father's mind.

"You."

That one word left Young Ham juggling a dozen scenarios. None felt right. He leaned back, keeping it cool, just in case Pop was fishing for something.

Ten minutes later, they pulled up to the duplex. Pop went straight to his room, shutting the door. Young Ham chilled on the couch, flipping channels until Pop called from the back.

Inside, Nika sat cross-legged on the bed, stacks of cash spread across the mattress. She counted bills with sharp fingers, barely glancing up before going right back to it. He supposed Pop was touching paper and dealing on another level, but seeing all that money laid out was different from imagining it—seeing was believing.

"Sit down," Pop told him.

Young Ham found a spot and sat.

Pop leaned on the bedframe, his face stone-cold. "So, you selling dope now."

Young Ham's chest tightened. *What? How did Pop find out already?* He tried keeping a poker face, saying nothing.

"Oh, so now you ain't got no words. But you been in the projects all night hustling."

Pop wasn't furious but he did look disappointed. His son had not only started selling, behind his back, but was grabbing work from God-knows-who. Worse, Pop had to hear it through the gossip vine. For him, their relationship was supposed to be solid. No reason for secrets.

"How much you sell? How long it take you to move it?" Pop asked.

"I bought a quarter around six yesterday after work. By seven, it was gone." Young Ham studied Pop's blank expression, hoping that was good enough.

Pop nodded at Nika. She zipped up a Nike gym bag stuffed with cash and handed him a sandwich bag of crack.

"How much this?" Pop asked.

"Come on, Pop, that's an ounce. I told you I copped a quarter yesterday. Four quarters make an ounce."

"Alright, now tell me what an ounce *posed* to weigh." Pop's tone wasn't just a question—it was a test.

Young Ham's throat went dry. "I think—"

"I don't want you to think," Pop cut in, voice rising. "I want you to tell me what a whole ounce weigh."

Young Ham's mind scrambled. He hated how empty his head felt. He shrugged, waving a white flag without saying it.

Pop cut him off sharp. "Men talk. Lil boys shrug their shoulders."

Heat flushed through Young Ham's chest. He hated how Pop's words cut, but they were true. He stammered, "My bad, Pop. I don't know."

Pop leaned back slightly, shaking his head. "That's cool. But game check, son. A straight-drop ounce is twenty-eight grams exact. No more, no less." He raised the circular ounce bag in his hand, letting the dim light glint off it like a trophy. "Day or night, that right there go for six hundred easy. If you dealing weight… you better know what weight class you in."

Young Ham listened. He wasn't just hearing numbers—he was hearing rules. A code. The kind of game that separated boys who played around from men who survived.

Then, just like that, Pop tossed the hard-white onto Young Ham's lap. The bag smacked against him, heavier than it looked, heavier than he expected. It was more than just dope—it was responsibility.

Caught off guard, Young Ham blurted, "Pop, I don't got six hundred."

"I never said you did." Pop shook his head. "Boy, yo mama gon' kill me if she find out I fronted you dope. But you chose this lane. You stepped in it."

Young Ham swallowed hard, gripping the bag like it might burn through his hands.

"Go get rid of that, bring back my money," Pop continued, his stare unblinking. "Then we'll talk about what's next. But hear me clear—don't ever keep that shit at yo granny's. Never crap where you nap."

The words carved into Young Ham, heavy as the dope on his lap. He nodded, but deep down, doubt twisted in his gut. This wasn't about moving weight—this was about proving himself, showing he could carry what Pop was handing him. And he wasn't sure if he was ready.

Six

Astonished at the sudden change of events, Young Ham stayed quiet the whole ride back to Maw-Maw's. His mind was racing. He pictured himself bossing up on the whole city, and opening the floodgates on Apt. 1301. With Pop sliding him work directly now, it was official—Young Ham had just inherited a pipeline. In other words, it was on.

The SL500 Benz rolled to a stop. Young Ham hopped out, shutting the door behind him. Nika tapped the horn twice before peeling down the street. Young Ham stretched and looked around. The abandoned house next door caught his attention. Plywood covered the windows, and the grass was wild like no one had cared for years.

Curious, he slid down the side of the house. The old Hispanic couple that used to live there were long gone—whether they died, moved, or just vanished, nobody seemed to know. What he did know was the place had been sitting untouched.

He wandered to the back. A raggedy wood frame shed leaned to the right, looking like one strong wind could drop it. At the bottom, he spotted a square hole big enough for a fist. He grinned. Perfect. Kneeling down, he tucked the ounce away inside, marking it as his personal stash until he came back with a razor blade.

Hopping the fence back to Maw-Maw's, he cut through the field by the old church, then walked to the store. He came back with a razor, a bag of Cool Ranch Doritos, and a blunt wrap for the loud Nika had left.

Inside the back room, Young Ham spread the work out on a chipped-up kitchen plate. He chopped the ounce into four quarters, then broke those down into dimes. His hands moved quick, precise, like he'd been doing it his whole life. By the end, he had a neat stack of 127 ten-dollar rocks. He bagged them into a Zip-Lock, then scraped the crumbs onto toilet paper for Liana. Nothing wasted.

Pop's words echoed in his head: if an ounce went for six hundred, doubling it meant twelve hundred minimum. No room for slip-ups. The re-up had to be exact.

Young Ham sat back, weighing the options. He couldn't risk moving it all. Too many things could go wrong—jackers, cops, or dumb luck. He pulled out sixty dimes, stuffed them in his pocket, and left the rest stashed. Better safe than sorry.

On his way up the hill, he swung by Ms. Joyce's apartment. Before he could knock, the door popped open and Stacks' younger brother stepped out.

"Sup, Young Ham?" Youngin' said, wiping his nose with the back of his hand.

"Ain't nothin', my nigg. Why you not in school?" Young Ham asked, side-eyeing him even though he knew he wasn't in class himself.

Youngin' smirked. "Man, fuck school. Them hoes called my momma, told her some shit I supposedly did last week. Now she trippin'."

Young Ham glanced down at Youngin's wrist, catching the shine. "Oh yeah? Where you get that watch?"

"Don't worry 'bout that, Young Ham," Youngin' grinned. "Just know a nigga stay laced."

They both cracked up, shaking their heads. Youngin' stayed suspended, and was always in trouble. School wasn't in his plans. To him, it was a waste of time and energy. Why sit in class when he could be on the block, running it up or taking what he wanted.

Young Ham had almost forgotten he came looking for Stacks when a fiend walked up, interrupting.

"Youngsters, y'all got some juice?"

Young Ham's whole vibe changed. He shot off the porch like a pit let off the leash. His voice boomed across the yard. "Do this look like a muthafuckin' crack house?"

He stopped inches from the fiend's face, finger almost touching his forehead. His jaw flexed, ready to flip him if he twitched wrong.

"I-I-I thought—" the geeker stammered, backing up.

"Wrong," Young Ham snapped, eyes blazing. "You thought wrong. Now get the fuck on before you can't walk at all."

The smoker stumbled back, shaking like he'd seen a ghost, then scampered away.

"Damn, Young Ham," Youngin' hollered, laughing so hard he bent at the waist. "You bold, my nigg."

Young Ham brushed his shirt straight. "Nah, homie. I ain't disrespecting yo T-Lady's spot. And I damn sure ain't lettin' no dope fiend bring heat to her doorstep. That's dead. By the way, where Stacks at?"

"Been grindin' in Wellington. You know he got that Gamine Girl droppin' big money on him." Youngin' said with a grin.

Young Ham nodded, but inside he wasn't feeling it. He knew how scandalous them chicks could be. Still, he couldn't knock Stacks for building his paper.

"Check it out, fam," Young Ham said, stepping down off the porch.

"I'm 'bout to blaze. Catch you on the rebound."

Youngin' nodded, gripping Young Ham's hand in their hood-shake. He held on tight. "This weak ass education shit fryin' me out, my nigga. I'm ready to get out there like you and my brother. Ready to make moves."

Young Ham locked eyes with him, firm. "Hold tight, hood. I got you."

Seven

Up the hill at Liana's, Young Ham slipped around back instead of knocking on the front door. He knew better. Five minutes later, Liana yanked open the door and went in on him.

"Young Ham, why the hell you beating on this door like you the damn law," she snapped. "Made me like to wet myself."

"Listen, we gotta start directing traffic to the back," Young Ham said, stepping inside and closing the door behind him. "The office got a clear view of the front. If the manager keeps seeing folks in and out, she gon' get suspicious and bring the laws down on us. How much it cost to get the lights turned on?"

He was tired of burning candles night after night.

"Last I checked, eighty dollars, I think."

Young Ham dug in his pocket, pulled out a crisp hundred, and pressed it into her hand. "Go see what's up while it's still early."

Liana threw on some clothes and headed out. Not five minutes later four licks pulled up and banged the front door. He let them in and served them, then laid down the new house rule.

"Listen close, and hear me well," he told them, his tone firm. "From now on, the front door is dead. Period. You want something, you come around back. That's the only way you get served."

37

He made it clear—no excuses, no exceptions. Anyone who broke that rule wasn't just losing their shot at dope, they'd be losing favor with him.

In the fifteen minutes Liana was gone, Young Ham cleared a hundred dollars. She came back later, hair frizzed and cursing up a storm.

"Them white bitches asking me all them damn questions like I was on trial. Bitch, I just want the lights on, not a damn job application. Whew! Come on here, Young Ham, I need to calm my nerves. Got damn devils done raised my blood pressure sky high."

He handed her a rock, laughing as she stormed upstairs.

"They said the lights supposed to be on by morning," she yelled back down.

Young Ham kept preaching the golden rule to anyone who didn't know. Over and over he drilled it: "Back door only." He studied faces, learned names, and spoke about things to come.

"Y'all let it be known far and wide," Young Ham told them. "If you fiendin' for that A-one, this is where it's at. Y'all can push that boo-boo in yo pipe all day if you want—that's on you. But if you want that drop? That's on me."

Pop's dope was strong enough to keep them coming. Young Ham knew it, and the regulars knew it. They called him Young Ham with respect, and praised the product. Some even asked if they could stay and smoke after copping. He left that to Liana. Her hospitality kept the customers loyal. She stayed high, they stayed supplied, and he never had to remind her of her role.

Then came the knock on the front door. There was always one.

Young Ham's blood boiled instantly. He stormed over, yanking it open with a scowl plastered across his face.

"What up, nigga?" he barked.

A young Hispanic dude stood there, cool as ice, acting like he didn't have a care in the world.

"Yo, I'm trying to get some work, dog," he said, as Young Ham sized him up.

"Nah, dog, I'm cool. Liana knows me."

That earned him a pass. Young Ham stepped back, allowing him inside.

"Hey, that yo' bike?"

"Yeh, bro."

"Alright, grab it and bring it too," Young Ham said, not trusting him to leave it outside.

He called Liana down to verify, praying she knew the dude. For his sake, she did. Young Ham's mood was lifted, but only slightly.

"Hey, mamas, I got eight dollars," Chico said, pulling crumbled bills from his pocket.

Chico's first mistake was coming short. But he hadn't learned house rules yet.

Young Ham broke it down in his head. Even if you gave your all but came up short, you still lost. Call it what you want but he wasn't doing business with short money.

"Look, Chico, I can't do nothing with that eight spot you got. Go find two more and holler at me."

"Dang, dog. What if I throw in my bike?"

The chrome Mongoose had black grips and fresh brakes, which sparked Young Ham's interest. He reckoned it could save time getting back and forth.

"Bet. Deal," Young Ham said. They swapped Chico's bike and eight bucks for three rocks.

Chico and Liana disappeared upstairs to smoke, and Young Ham called back, "Liana, I'll be back. Lock up." He grabbed the new ride and shot out the door.

It was 3:30, hot, and the streets baked under the sun. Young Ham pedaled past the basketball court. His chest tightened when a powder-blue Jumpout Boy's van bent the corner on Bedford and slid in the Bricks.

"Stop now!" Undercover officer Bridges barked from the sliding door.

Young Ham glared back but kept riding. Bridges' reputation was all brutality, but Young Ham wasn't about to fold.

The van's motor roared. "Screeeech!" It skidded to a halt ahead of him. Bridges and his partner Potato-Head leapt out, charging. Before he knew it, he was yanked up and slammed inside the van. His poor bike lay flying in the grass, wheels spinning.

Inside, Bridges drove a fist into his gut. Air exploded from Young Ham's chest. He curled up, wheezing.

"Where's the dope at, you punk?" Potato-Head snarled, flipping Young Ham's pockets inside out. He found the eight dollars Chico gave him and threw it in his face.

"Broke dick hustler."

Young Ham kept most of his money stashed in his shoes for moments like this. His eyes burned with anger, but he knew better—one wrong move meant more punishment.

"I think I saw him swallow something," the driver lied, fueling Bridges' rage.

"Spit it out, muthafucka. Spit it out!" Bridges roared, choking Young Ham by the throat. He writhed, lungs on fire, barely able to breathe.

The dirty cops gave in, figuring he must have tossed the drugs off him.

"When I do get you, and you best believe I will—you ain't ever gon' fuck with me again," Bridges growled, punctuating his words with another gut shot.

Young Ham's last breath escaped. Bridges and Potato-Head dumped him out on the pavement and peeled off.

He lay there wheezing, gathering strength. Slowly, he dragged himself to his bike, coasted the rest of the way to Maw-Maw's, and stumbled inside.

"Baby, your mama called looking for you," Maw-Maw said, eyes narrowing. "What's the matter?"

"I'm fine, nothing," he muttered, heading straight for the kitchen phone. Don't ask why Maw-Maw still had a landline in the kitchen, but she did.

Mom picked up on the first ring. "Boy, you can't call and check on your mama no more?" she said, her voice sharp but full of love.

"Mama, you know it ain't like that. I just been busy." The lie felt heavy even as it left his lips.

"Busy doing what, that I can't have none of your time."

"Working at the shop with Pop," he lied again, hating how weak it sounded.

"Hmmm. So when you coming by?" she asked in that tone only mamas got, a question that was really a command. "I'm making enchiladas tomorrow."

Young Ham smiled despite his aches. Mom knew what bait to use. She knew he couldn't pass up her enchiladas.

"Ma, I'ma make sure I get there. You just have them ready."

They both laughed and hung up.

<h1 style="text-align:center">Eight</h1>

Despite shaking off the run-in with the blue boys, Young Ham's heart still hammered in his chest like a bass drum. His lungs burned and each breath was sharp as glass. His nerves buzzed like live wires, and the dirty cop's voices echoed in his head long after they were gone.

Fear had been right there, sitting heavy in his gut, but pride wouldn't let him admit it. What scared him more than the cops was the thought of slipping, getting caught sloppy, and letting down Pop. *You can't hustle scared,* he reminded himself, but the truth was he was shook—angry that the law had that kind of grip on him.

That close call branded him. It was a reminder—the hustle wasn't a game; one slip could cost him everything. From now on, at the first slight of a badge, he was gone. No hesitation, no second-guessing. Young Ham swore on it; he'd never let them boys catch him slipping again.

Young Ham kicked off his shoes, pulling money from the stash hidden in the sole. Inside the closet, shoeboxes were stacked to the ceiling. He tucked six hundred dollars away for Pop, then slid the box back at the bottom of the shelf.

To avoid waking Maw-Maw from her midday nap, Young Ham slipped quietly out the side door. He grabbed the rest of the dope from the neighbor's yard and hopped on his bike to finish the grind. Chico was still hanging around when he got back, and Young Ham could sense Chico and Liana were more than smoking buddies.

Same as before, the block wasted no time running through his crack sack. A few newcomers needed the pep-talk, but most buyers knew house rules and flowed through the back door accordingly.

That changed when a knock rattled the front screen. Young Ham knew he had to stand on his word and set the example. He peeked out the window. It was Jimbone, a middle-aged smoker who accepted the rules but decided to test them.

When Young Ham yanked the door open, Jimbone stood there looking careless, like he wasn't on the hotseat. He had violated; so it didn't matter what excuse he had. Before Jimbone could speak, a three-piece combo buckled his knees. Young Ham followed with a devastating hook to the ribs, folding him on impact. Jimbone gasped for air, tried to apologize, but a six-inch uppercut put him out cold.

Disrespecting a man's word was the foulest move. Pop had drilled that into him. *Always mean what you say, so you can always say what you mean.* Young Ham had seen Pop demand respect from some of the grimiest dudes alive, and he wanted that same esteem for himself.

He sent Jimbone stumbling down the block, eyes swollen, body sore, and spirit broken. As he headed inside, Young Ham could feel eyes on him—a watchful stare burning from across the way where Crystal stayed. Everybody in the hood called her Juicy, thanks to her lips, hips, and ass.

Juicy was undeniable. Her beauty and hood-rat swag kept random dudes posted outside her spot, and today was no different. Leaning on her porch was a semi-fat, light-skinned outsider. By the looks of him, he wasn't from the Bricks. Not dressed like that. He had on a throwback Mitchell & Ness Emmitt Smith jersey, black-and-blue Foam Posites with laced blue guts, and a solid blue rag draped across his shoulder. A clear sign he was banging for the other side.

Young Ham stared him down, but he knew set-tripping held no future. He represented his environment, true enough, and if that meant riding for the hood solo, so be it. He broke the stare first. He went back inside positive that he and Little Boy Blue were doomed to crash, especially if the outsider kept popping up at Juicy's.

"Liana, I'ma get at you tomorrow when I come back with some more work," Young Ham said, finishing his last sale.

"You should've saved me something if you knew you wasn't coming back," Liana shouted from upstairs, heated. "What kind of shit is that, Young Ham?"

"I got you tomorrow. Now come lock the door, woman," he replied, shutting it behind him as she kept fussing.

Once again, Young Ham abandoned his duty post. How could he neglect his spot and expect it to float? Dope fiends stalled out when dealers ran dry, and once they found out Apt. 1301 was topped out, off toward the next man holding a sack.

But Pop had only fronted him one zone, and that was history. It was clear what Pop supplied was in demand, and he needed more than one. Enough to hold down a hard-hustling shift. He thought about hollering at Fat Mack for a quick flip, but killed the thought. No sense provoking Pop into another uproar.

He hopped on his bike and rolled over to the apartment building where his homie Lil Nate and his sister Toya stayed. Their mom, Jewel, was smoked out—one of those careless addicts only worried about the next hit. Many times, Lil Nate and Toya were left alone for hours, even days, fending for themselves.

Young Ham didn't pity them. He knew plenty of hustlers who grew up the same or worse. Still, he had a soft spot for them, especially Lil Nate, who was already showing signs of becoming a warrior. Young Ham helped whenever he could, promising new kicks for good grades and keeping them laced with little things to make life lighter.

As usual, Jewel's apartment door was wide open, and she was nowhere to be found.

"Look out Lil Nate… Toya,"

Young Ham called as he stepped inside.

Footsteps scattered on the stairs. Lil Nate was first down—tall and lanky, buck teeth from sucking his thumb. Every time Young Ham caught him at it, he'd punch him in the chest and make him push-up until his arms and legs trembled. Toya stumbled close behind, cheesing.

"Where you been, Young Ham?" Lil Nate asked, hugging him tight.

"What up lil' man? You still suckin' yo' thumb?" Young Ham stepped back for a good look. If Lil Nate dropped his head, he was lying.

"That ain't what playas do," Lil Nate shot back, chin high with pride, repeating words Young Ham recited awhile back.

Young Ham grinned. "Alright then, gimme some dap." They ran their handshake—though Lil Nate always fumbled it.

"I know whoever name Toya better come give Young Ham a hug before it be a problem," Young Ham teased.

Toya crept forward bashfully, grinning ear to ear. She was the opposite of Lil Nate—where he was boot black, she was high yellow with long curly hair.

The second she got close, Young Ham pounced, tickling her until she screamed and lost balance. She laughed hard, struggling to escape. Lil Nate leapt on Young Ham's back yelling, "Get off my sister! Get off my sister!"

Before long, Young Ham had them both pinned on a dirty laundry pile, squealing until they surrendered.

"Listen up," he said, serious now. "This door always open. Anybody can walk in anytime. If y'all ever need me—Lil Nate, you the oldest—you come get me at Liana's. Y'all hear me?"

"Can we go to the store, Young Ham?" Lil Nate asked.

"Yeah, please, Young Ham," Toya added.

Young Ham scribbled a note for Jewel, letting her know they'd gone to the store. Lord knew he didn't need her tripping, calling the laws, or breaking down if she came back and found them gone.

Jewel was still missing when they returned. No surprise there. Every time Young Ham visited, he ended up leaving Lil Nate and Toya alone. Each time he walked away, it felt like he was abandoning them—but what else could he do?

Nine

Testing season on the streets came and went. You either stayed ready or got folded and left curbside. Young Ham was up early, knocking out push-ups and crunches, then he showered and dressed. He sat on the edge of the bed, studying and restacking yesterday's earnings—$1,210. Not bad, considering the short grind.

Hollering at Pop about leveling up his workload was a priority. Pop was once a block hustler himself, so Young Ham knew he wouldn't deny the grind. If anything, he'd do nothing but respect the go-getter effort, bless his game, and extend more than enough this go around.

Then came Mom. He had avoided her presence since jumping headfirst into the lifestyle. She was the last person he expected not to notice the change. She'd see right through the bravado of hitting late nights and getting quiet money. When he dropped by later, he promised himself he'd keep it honest—but only if she asked.

"Good morning," Young Ham said, stepping into the kitchen and greeting one of the most prominent women in his life.

"Hey, baby," she replied, tilting her head to catch his kiss. "Your daddy called to see were you up."

"What he want?"

"Boy, I don't know. He didn't say."

Maw-Maw was tough as old leather, and stubborn as they came. Even in her eighties, she moved around well using a metal walker, spirit still motherly-strong. After eating, Young Ham cleaned the kitchen and washed dishes. As he stacked the last plate, underneath his feet trembled. A low rumble shook the window panes. Pop had pulled up in his Buick, praised on the streets as "King-Kong" since winning Best Quality Sound at the Texas Heat Wave.

"What's happenin', Pop?" Young Ham greeted, holding the screen open.

"Hey, boy, where yo' grandma at?" Pop asked, towering in the doorway, six-foot-four, wide as a doorframe from years of weights and work.

"She in her room. Probably on the phone with Aunt Carmen." Young Ham slid onto the couch while Pop rapped with Maw-Maw. He sat rehearsing in his head how he'd bring up the conversation about getting Pop's approval on pushing his hustle days forward.

Lil Wayne's *Carter* CD rattled the Buick like a war drum. Young Ham rode shotgun, bobbing his head as they cruised toward MLK and Springdale. Pop cut the music, frowned at the Shell's parking lot, and whipped the car in fast. Something was off about the crowded gas station.

Parked in front of the automatic air pump and payphones, a candy-red Suburban blasted loud music, entertaining the crowd. Pop stepped out, left the car running, and brushed shoulders on his way through. The displeased crowd whispered about the barrel-chested man breaking up their meet and greet.

From the passenger seat, Young Ham stiffened. Eyes locked on Pop. No flinch, no blink. Pop linked with a diamond-dripped D-boy and engaged in conversation. Then, in a blink, Pop dropped him cold, sliding him three feet across the pavement like a rag doll. He napped on the side of his Suburban. The party ended. People scattered and dove into their vehicles, fleeing the pandemonium. No one wanted part in the potential threat if they stuck around longer. His partners froze, stuck in disbelief, until Pop raised his shirt, flashing a chrome .357 King Cobra in the sunlight.

"What y'all niggas wanna do?" Pop barked.

They didn't.

One by one, they peeled off, leaving their man stretched out.

When Pop slid back into the driver's seat, still burning hot. He turned to Young Ham. "If a nigga owe you something—you go take it. If you think a nigga owe you something—you go take it."

He dropped the Buick in gear, boosted the bang, and hung the dude's platinum piece and chain on the rearview mirror. The lesson burned itself into Young Ham's chest.

Ten

Young Ham sat there frozen, but it wasn't fear holding him still—it was awe. The chain swinging from the mirror gleamed like a crown jewel, proof that Pop's word was bond. "If a nigga owe you something… you go take it."

He replayed it over and over, committing it to memory. He wanted that same edge, that same aura that made grown men back down without a fight. He straightened in his seat, eyes burning with a new kind of focus. The game wasn't just about money anymore. It was about standing tall, about demanding your place and making sure nobody could take it from you. Pop continued sharpening Young Ham's game as they cruised the hilly streets of the ATX. "Son, you play for victory only. If you not winning, you gots to be losing. Slow money better than po'money, and that's better than no' money any day."

Young Ham soaked up the free game. Pop's mentorship set him apart from peers his age. Whether good or bad, not many had influencing father figures. Thanks to Pop, Young Ham possessed a legitimate game.

When they pulled up at Pop's spot, Young Ham found himself seated where Pop handed over his first ounce. He was mid-sentence about how Apt. 1301 had turned up in a short time. Pop stopped him cold, holding up a finger.

"How much money you got right now?"

Twelve hundred and ten dollars," Young Ham replied, laying the bills on the dresser so Pop could see.

"Count it out."

Young Ham counted slow and precise. Pop's eyes narrowed.

"How long it take you to make that?"

"No more than three hours tops," Young Ham said, proud.

"All from this one apartment you been braggin' on?"

"Yep."

Pop's tone flipped like a switch, his face hardened. "Take this serious. You barred from stepping foot in this house again… even for pizza."

The words hit harder than a slap. Young Ham sat there confused until Nika handed him a slick black cell phone.

"Business only," Pop instructed. "Nika runnin' supply and demand. When you sell out, you hit her. Nothin' else. No extra talking. Learn code like it's nine to five. Even then, keep it short."

From there, Nika drove him to Pinky's and had the phone activated under a fake ID. Young Ham recapped all that unfolded. Pop failed at mentioning the amount of dope he had coming, nor did he say when. He only warned again to keep nothing at his mother's house.

Before getting out of the car, Nika hit Young Ham with a wink. "Answer the phone, tomorrow."

By the time he hit the porch at home, Young Ham felt like a million bucks—money in his pocket, new phone, new pager, and a fresh connection on unlimited re-up. He was moving up.

Pop had reimbursed the $1,200 owed as front money, telling Young Ham don't sweat it. He wasn't. From his bankroll, he separated $210 and put the other thousand aside, then went and called Stacks.

"Where you at, bro?" "I'm bending corners… talk to me."

Young Ham could barely hear over the blasting music. "Yo, pull up on me. I'm on Goodwin."

"That's a bet."

Stacks swung the block in a burgundy, chrome-trimmed Cadillac Eldorado Biarritz. Young Ham hopped in and exchanged dap.

"I see you, boy."

"Nah, fam. This my bitch whip. I'm just making moves," Stacks said, brushing it off. He was down for tearing into Mom's enchiladas. Once they burned the swisher, they were heading straight over.

"Peep this," Young Ham said. "I laid the law on a tweaker behind talking me lightly. Then some fool at Juicy's mugged me like I ain't belong."

"Man, I'm fed up with these off-brand clowns. Ain't nothing friendly 'bout the East. I'ma start knocking shit out."

"I'm wit all that, no doubt," Young Ham said calmly. "But we 'bout that paper first. We reppin' the biggest dope-infested projects in the city. Ain't no way we shouldn't be ballin'. Tomorrow, I'ma link everybody up."

The two laughed about how Young Ham crushed Jimbone, then Stacks raised the sound system and played Z-Ro's new CD. By the time they reached Mom's, she was standing at the door, smiling wide.

"There go my baby," she said, kissing Young Ham's forehead and leaving a make-up smear he wiped away quickly. "Jamal, is that you? Boy, come hug me. Standing there like you don't know nobody."

Stacks hugged and kissed Mom's cheek. "Y'all come on. I just finished cooking." Mom prepared plates like they hadn't seen a meal in days. "Foreal Colleck Junior," she called as he and Stacks dug into their plates greedily. Young Ham knew it was serious. She only used his full name and *that* tone when her heart was heavy.

He found Mom leaning against the dresser, arms folded tight across her chest. Her face was soft but stressful, like she was holding the world on her shoulders. He caught the shimmer of tears at the corners of her eyelids.

"Mama, what's wrong?" he asked, his voice low. She took a deep breath before answering, almost like she didn't want to let the words out.

"Baby… I'm worried about you." Her voice dropped to a whisper. "You be careful out there. I just… I just want you safe."

Young Ham nodded, but the way she looked at him made his chest ache. She reached out and smoothed his cheek, her hand trembling just a little.

"I'm prayin' you get everything you looking for in life," she said, fighting the tears.

Her words hung heavy in the room. It was more of a heartbreak than a lecture. A mother realizing her boy had slipped too far into the streets, and there wasn't much she could do but pray.

Eleven

The following day kicked off with a bang. Nika pulled up early, cranking the Motorola to life at six a.m. sharp. Young Ham slipped out the side door, meeting her out front. She rolled the window down when she spotted him cutting the corner of the house.

"You hungry?" she asked, handing him two What-A-Burger bags.

"Starving!" he said, gripping the bags like treasure.

"Eat up then." she said, before peeling off down the block. Young Ham stood there puzzled at how quick she moved.

The first bag he opened was still warm, filled with breakfast. He opened the second — and froze, dropping it to the ground after seeing ounces stacked on top of ounces. His heart jumped. He wasted no time snatching up the sack, and hustling it underneath the shed, hiding the bag and all.

Back inside, he tossed the breakfast tacos and cinnamon rolls in the fridge for later. The hunger in his stomach couldn't match the hunger for power and wealth.

Pop had done the unexpected that morning, handing down a quarter-kilo already cooked and ready. Sixteen years old and holding that much weight was no small thing. But if Pop believed he could manage it, Young Ham was ready to prove him right.

Sleep came quick after. When he woke, his mind was already spinning.

Seven three-hour shifts needed filling, positions assigned for moving crack rocks in the Bricks. Without missing a beat, Young Ham showered, ate, and got to it.

"I'll be back later, Maw-Maw," he called as she stayed glued to *The Price Is Right*.

He left his bike behind and hit the block on foot, searching for the homies who carried the same fire for money as he did — maybe even more.

First stop was Youngin's crib. Young Ham knew if anybody would ride, it was him. Youngin' was already on the porch when Young Ham strolled up.

"Young Ham, what's the deal? I see you up early on the hunt."

"Actually, I came to scream at you. Sit down and ride with me," Young Ham said, throwing an arm over his shoulder as they caught the edge of Ms. Joyce's porch.

"Today we 'bout to form an alliance built on hood love and stacking ends," Young Ham began. "What I want for myself is what I want for my niggas. If we come together and don't let greed tear us apart, we can lock this shit down for ourselves. So, you on board or what?"

Youngin' raised his head, met Young Ham's eyes, and nodded. "Fuck yeah, I'm boarding the mothership. About time shit woke up 'round here."

Young Ham led the way over to where Killa and his sister Porsha stayed.

Killa was the smallest in the clique, and carried a serious little-man complex. He snapped at any testing or teasing, and never backed down.

He spotted them before they hit the porch, sliding out the screen door. Killa flashed the hood sign proudly. Young Ham and Youngin' answered the praise alike, and after a round of daps they settled near the porch steps.

"So, you on board or what?" Young Ham asked, rattling off his final words.

Killa stretched, yawning, "Shid, what we waitin' on? Let's get this money." He ducked back inside, reappearing with a deuce-deuce pistol tucked in his back pocket. "If you ain't packin'... you lackin'."

They moved on to scoop Smiley. He was an old man's baby, rocking a goatee and already showing signs of going bald. His pops, Old Man Dean, was sixty-five, grumpy as hell, and always griped about white folks. He loved wetting his porch and stopping them from hanging out.

Smiley leaned out his upstairs window when he heard the pebbles being thrown. They all raised their hands. A second later, he crawled out, dropped off the roof, and landed light on his feet.

From there, they walked a couple buildings down and gathered in Liana's kitchen, smoke circling as blunts got passed. Liana had recently added some secondhand furniture and a used microwave from the flea market and pawn shop. She even snagged a rinky-dink A/C unit to keep the heat down.

Young Ham laid out the play once again for Smiley's ears. It didn't take much convincing. Smiley was down with whatever fattened his pockets.

Now all that was left was waiting on Stacks. Truth was, the clique hadn't squaded up like this in a long minute, and it felt good. Young Ham let the moment settle in.

When Stacks finally showed, he stepped in, gave the room one long look, and caught the meaning instantly. His eyes misted a little as the weight of the meeting hit home.

Although the vibe was alive, Young Ham knew the real business had to come first. "Beside me," he said, breaking the silence, "who else trying to make a name and put the hood on they back?"

Hands went up, voices overlapping, everybody wanting a piece of the conversation.

Stacks leaned in. "Too many new faces out here runnin' wild, making shit hot."

"Shit outta control if you ask me," Killa threw in.

"Order gotta be enforced if we want real growth," Smiley added, sounding like a damn bookworm.

Youngin' clapped his hands. "Between five heads trying to eat off one block, ain't no leftovers for outsiders nibbling on crumbs."

"Exactly," Young Ham nodded. "So if you ain't part of this brotherhood but think you can eat off this land anyway, you're violating street code zero-point-two…and that violation is punishable up to death."

Twelve

Two Months Later

"Youngster, y'all keep that fire!" Josephine hollered, a periodic smoker who lived on the office-side in Apt. 701. Her son Lil Larry and Lil Nate played ball together and were tight.

In no time, Young Ham and the squad had the Bricks in a chokehold. They flipped countless ounces at max rate, stuffing untaxed cash into shoeboxes until they overflowed.

Getting fronted himself, Young Ham flipped it forward to his crime partners for seven hundred a zip. Ounces — better known on the block as "zips" — moved quick. He broke down the all-dime cutting system and drilled it into the crew, making sure they followed. The profits came heavy and steady.

Shifts were locked in tight and rostered accordingly. Everybody played their role. Young Ham and Stacks doubled up since five solid heads were ready, and seven bodies were needed to keep the block hot.

Young Ham worked the morning grind from six to nine, then doubled back from nine to noon. Stacks slid in from twelve to three. Youngin' grabbed the wheel from three to six. Killa covered six to nine, while Smiley — always slick — snuck out for the nine to midnight stretch, crawling back through the window before Old Man Dean stirred. Stacks closed out the graveyard; his whip access let him maze wherever needed.

The hustle never slowed. When the streets noticed record-breaking crack sales from sun-up to sun-down, the city began whispering. The only thing louder than the hustle was the reason behind it: money.

Young Ham's stash swelled over the months, and was climbing. He'd stacked ten bands in hundreds alone, but doubt crept in. Anyone could break in and strip him of the fat shoeboxes stacked high inside the closet. He knew a safer spot was a must.

"My nigga," Young Ham said, dapping Stacks as he stepped in before shift change. "Right on time. I just finished."

"Sometime its scary how fast this shit be moving." Stacks grinned, bumping fists. "Yo Pop got a nigga ahead."

"No doubt," Young Ham nodded. "We just gotta mash and keep the leeches off our block."

Out of habit, Young Ham glanced out the window. Little Boy Blue, the same fool from the stare-down a few days back — was bold enough to be short-stopping right in front of their building.

Young Ham's blood boiled. Rage rose quick. Nothing cut deeper than another man eating off your plate.

"Say pat'na," Young Ham said, storming toward him. "What you think you doing?"

"Yo, cuz," Little Boy Blue shot back, standing his ground. "I don't owe you or no other nigga no explanation."

Those words sounded like the bell in a boxing ring. Young Ham was already charging, destruction roaring in his chest. Little Boy Blue swung sloppy. Young Ham weaved and unleashed a lightning-fast combination. Little Boy Blue stumbled but caught his balance, firing wild haymakers back.

Young Ham ducked low, rolling under the sloppy swings. A sharp step left gave him an angle, and he cracked Little Boy Blue with a body shot followed by a stiff uppercut. Little Boy Blue stumbled sideways, guard wide open.

Bad intentions were in Young Ham's eyes as he closed in. Little Boy Blue fumbled in his waistband, digging for something he never reached.

When out of nowhere, Stacks appeared, and crushed Little Boy Blue with an overhand that sent him crashing, laid out cold on the pavement.

They stomped him into the dirt until an old lady screamed from her porch. "Y'all leave that boy alone!"

Breathing heavy, Young Ham ripped the Sig-Sauer from Little Boy Blue's shorts, staring at the steel. He swallowed dryly, knowing how close he'd come to being shot — maybe killed. If Stacks hadn't shown up, it could've been him in the dirt.

That day marked a change. Young Ham forbade himself from moving reckless, never wanting to be caught slipping or labeled a victim. From then on, pistol-packing became his new hobby.

Later That Evening...

The squad huddled at Liana's before heading down to Rosewood Park, Wednesday's hotspot. A local rapper sponsored the event called *Jump-On-It*, that drew every teenager for blocks.

"Man, what's the point of standing at some corny park when we could be chasing dough?" Smiley complained, displeased the squad was sliding without him.

"Somebody gotta hold down the block, hood," Young Ham replied, knowing Smiley just hated crowds. Ever since he started bubbling on the grind, the money pulled him deeper. If Old Man Dean ever found out, it might kill him.

"Ah, shut up with that anti-social shit," Youngin' instigated. "I'm trying to snatch a chicken-butt from across town. These Eastside hoes ain't it."

"Yeah, whatever," Smiley smirked. "A hoe off the East will whoop a bitch from anywhere else. Plus, I'ma have yo shift while you gon', goofy."

Their bickering turned to slap-boxing until Liana stormed down the stairs. "Goddammit! Take that shit outside! Not in my house!"

"Y'all chill," Stacks said, cutting in. "Smiley, hold it down 'til we back."

"Yes indeed," Smiley grinned wide as the Grand Canyon.

At the park, the scene was football stadium packed. Cars lined every street. Getting a decent parking spot meant either coming early or circling the blocks for show. Barbecue pits smoked, while the Hater Haterz, a local rap group, lit up the stage.

Young Ham pushed through the shoulder-rubbing crowd until he spotted her — Kamiko. Fine as ever, she rocked a spaghetti-strap top and stone-washed jeans that hugged her curves. She had every dude in the park double-taking.

"Hey, y'all, I'm 'bout to bust a move. I got a rose to pick," Young Ham told the clique, slipping away before they could clown him.

He dipped into the sea of bodies, coming up behind her smooth, wrapping his arms around Kamiko's waist. He pulled her close, her Bath & Body Works scent hitting his nose. ."You miss me?" he whispered, lips brushing her ear.

Kamiko stiffened, then twisted quick, her small fist landing on his chest. "Where you been, Young Ham? And why haven't you been back to school?"

He rubbed the spot, wincing but smiling. "Dang, girl, slow down. You out here swinging like I ain't just bless you with my presence. I got expelled, remember? But if you was mine, I never would've left."

"Don't play, Young Ham," she teased, pushing him back. "You know I had a boyfriend."

"Had," he shot back.

She folded her arms, trying to front, but a little smile betrayed her. "Yes... had. We broke up. I don't mess with him no more."

Young Ham's grin spread wide. He took her hand and spun her around, pulling her into his chest when she came back around.

"So what you saying? This all me now?"

She laughed, shaking her head, but didn't pull away. "Boy, you crazy."

Thirteen

Young Ham had done the honor of making Kamiko his girl. To him, it wasn't about having a pretty face on his arm. It was about finding somebody who made him want to slow his roll, in a world that never stopped moving.

Whenever a hustling break presented itself, he'd slide across town to her side. Kamiko stayed northwest, in a spread-out neighborhood far from the chaos of the Bricks—no dice games on the corner, no sirens blaring every hour—just quiet streets.

At times when Young Ham didn't catch a cab, Youngin' would drop him off in a dope fiend's rental car he kept handy. Kamiko didn't care if he showed up in a Benz or a bucket, long as it was him. He'd climb inside her window, and she'd be waiting with a smile that cooled all the fire he kept bottled up.

They'd sit on her bed, legs tangled, talking about everything and nothing. She'd ask him questions nobody else thought to: *Did he ever think about life outside the block? Did he ever wish he didn't have to carry a pistol just to feel safe?* He didn't always answer, but she made him think.

One morning, while on shift, a red-tinted Lexus LS on 17s cut through the Bricks. The driver was Keno from Cedar Block, an 02 set on the East known as Blood territory.

Keno had grown up in the projects at the bottom of the hill with his mom and two sisters. Both parents were seasoned crack addicts, so the game came early for him. He'd seen the struggle firsthand and swore that when he came up, he'd never look back.

He met Bubba in middle school. Bubba took him to his hood, the Cedar Block, and showed him the ropes. The two became inseparable, stacking paper like it grew on trees. But it all ended when Bubba got shot in the chest by a pair of penny-pinching robbers.

After Bubba's death, Keno got with Bubba's sister, Poocey. He was crazy, and she was crazier. She blessed him with a kilo Bubba left behind, and it was a wrap.

"What's the haps, family?" Keno grinned, flashing a mouthful of gold and VVS diamonds. Young Ham had come around the back when he caught the sound of music thumping from out front.

"You got it, homie," Young Ham said, slapping fives with one of the originals. Keno had heard about Young Ham and the boys making noise and crawled through to show love.

"On the real, y'all lil niggas got this bitch sewed up. I like that," Keno pointed out, nodding his respect.

"Word," Young Ham said. "They say if you ain't being talked about... you ain't doing nothing," he added. Both laughed, knowing it was the messy truth.

"Look here, young gee. I'ma catch you boys in traffic. Stay up 'til you come up, and when you come up... stay down. Holler if you need me."

After dapping Keno, Young Ham started to head around back. That's when Lil Nate came running up fast, breathless and wide-eyed.

"Young Ham! Young Ham!" he said, tugging Young Ham's arm.

On one side, Lil Nate's face was swollen like he'd been punched.

Young Ham's gun was out and ready. Whoever did this to his lil homie was getting it on sight.

"Come on, Young Ham! That man got Toya!" Lil Nate pleaded, yanking harder.

Young Ham broke out full speed toward Jewel's spot. Toya's scream cut through the air as he flew through the door, taking stairs two at a time. At the top, he froze in the doorway. A dirty white man sprawled on top of Toya's twelve-year-old body.

"Get yo bitch ass off her!" Young Ham barked, pistol locked in his grip. The intruder rolled over, and Young Ham's blood turned cold — it was crackhead Jimbone.

"Fuck you, nigger!" Jimbone snarled, teeth rotten, breath foul. Toya curled up on the bed crying in agony, her Winnie the Pooh panties ripped and stained red.

Boom... boom... boom... Three shots tore through Jimboare's chest and dropped him violently. He hit the floor face-down, drowning in a pool of his own blood.

Police and EMS dragged their feet showing up. Paramedics rushed Toya to the ER once they realized she'd been assaulted. Lil Nate got taken into CPS custody while investigators drilled Young Ham about Jewel and the abandoned kids. Even after all that, there was still no sign of Jewel.

Medical staff didn't bother with Jimboare — he'd been dead for hours.

As for Young Ham, he left Jewel's in cuffs. He'd stuck around for Lil Nate and Toya's sake, but now he was on his way to juvenile.

APD drove him in the back of a squad car to Gardner-Betts, the juvenile center on the Southside. After booking, they placed him in the "Gladiator dorm," where all the violent cases went. First day in, Young Ham stayed calm, blending with youngsters fighting for clout all around him. He itched to make an example out of someone looking to score points off him.

Mom came to visit. She couldn't process the thought of her son locked on a murder rap. At visitation, her words began and ended with Jesus.

Young Ham tried to ease her worries, swearing he'd be alright. But she couldn't shake the fear, like her son was already buried underneath the jail. Deep down, she realized the boy she raised was no longer, and Young Ham — whom the streets birthed — was alive and well.

Pop showed up a week later and brought Ed Dickerson, a top defense lawyer out of Round Rock, Texas. Young Ham listened to Mr. Dickerson, but his eyes stayed on Pop. Pop's calm nature was all he needed. If Pop wasn't sweating, neither would he.

As the attorney wrapped up the court game plan, Pop finally spoke, "Try to stay outta trouble, boy." Then, sternly, he added, "Don't talk to nobody about what happened… and I mean not a soul."

Fourteen

Time at Gardner-Betts went smoother than Young Ham expected. No major drama crossed his path. Most dudes inside respected his name, and his outside rep carried enough weight to keep trouble at bay. The rest were small-time hustlers, wishing they had the same shine. Long as everybody stayed in their lane, Young Ham had no reason to trip.

Still, going back and forth to court twice a month wore on him. The lawyer Pop hired stayed in touch, week after week. Mr. Dickerson argued that the judge's focus on a sixteen-year-old caught with a pistol was overblown, making Young Ham wonder what planet she lived on. Everybody packed heat—how could she single him out like some kind of menace?

Young Ham figured the judge had no clue what it was like outside her gated community. Maybe if she stepped into the trenches, she'd understand why a young man like him needed a pistol in arm's reach. Until then, she had no say.

Most of Young Ham's days inside were simple—reading, working out, keeping to himself. He didn't waste time on board games or gossip. Kamiko wrote weekly, promising she missed him badly and couldn't wait for his release. Her mother wasn't so kind, always pushing her to cut ties. To get around that, he had to sneak letters out through friends who still went to school with her.

Then came another court date. This time it was serious—the real deal, according to Mr. Dickerson. That morning, Young Ham was walked by two staff members to the detention center's courtroom. He expected flashing cameras and reporters hungry to ask about the murder. Instead, only the judge, his attorney, Mom, and Pop were there.

From the moment he sat beside Mr. Dickerson, time sped up—making him think he'd missed something. He glanced at Mom's tear-streaked face and felt a sharp sting of guilt. Pop, solid as always, hit him with a thumbs up and a fist pump. Mr. Dickerson patted his shoulder before the staff reappeared to lead him out.

The elevator ride back to his dorm was quiet. Young Ham slumped against the wall feeling like he drifted through fog. Mr. Dickerson's words, Mom's tears, Pop's signal—all played back in his head. But when that steel door slammed shut behind him, the weight of it all hit like a ton of bricks.

The judge handed down twelve months in the Texas Youth Commission. She mentioned something about good behavior getting him out in nine months. Whatever else came from her wrinkled mouth was drowned by thoughts of him rushing the bench, and slapping the dentures straight out her mouth.

Didn't she know I'm the King of the Bricks? Didn't she know I got a whole operation waiting on me? A year gone could cost me everything.

Still, Young Ham did the math. If he rode the whole year out, which he probably would, he'd manage. No sense stressing the "what-ifs." He had money stashed. Ten tucked in the attic at Mom's, and another fifteen in big faces buried under Maw-Maw's house. Nobody was digging that up anytime soon.

Young Ham wasn't sure where he'd land once he got to TYC, but one thing was guaranteed—his presence would be felt. Even if they launched him to the moon, folks would still know his name.

$ $ $ $ $

The van ride to TYC felt endless. Shackled wrist-to-wrist with Seven, Young Ham stared out the window, mind grinding through what was ahead. Seven, a rowdy southsider from Dove Springs, stayed loud the whole trip, spitting gang talk and making it clear trouble wasn't far behind him.

"I know these crab niggas gon' try to make me lay down my flag," Seven said, teeth flashing in a grin that didn't match the heat in his eyes. "But I'm comin' home red, or I'm comin' home dead."

Young Ham bumped his fist against Seven's free hand. "Hold it down, if you don't do nothing else. If it go down in my presence, I already told you—I'm ridin'. City come first."

Seven nodded. "Bet that."

By the time Young Ham blinked awake from a half-sleep, the van slowed. Out the window, a faded sign announced the Youth Commission's State School—a place with a rep for being one of the toughest, most violent lockups in the state.

He stepped off the van to a wall of hard stares. He knew the look: eyes searching, sizing him up, hunting for weakness. He gave none back. Walking across the yard felt like stepping into a battlefield where everybody waited to see if he'd fold.

From the jump, guards acted tough, barked orders, and wore no-nonsense masks on their faces. Other boys, most around his age, locked eyes with him, hungry for a test. Young Ham didn't flinch. He had already learned that letting someone think you were soft was the first step to becoming prey.

During intake, they assigned him a living unit. The second he walked through, it felt like every stare glued to him, like "sucker" had been stamped across the back of his jumper. He smirked anyway, unfazed.

"Look out, homeboy," a tall, brown-skinned dude stepped up, testing him. "Where you from?"

"My name Young Ham. I'm from ATX. Eastside."

"Nigga, I don't nobody give a fuck 'bout that baloney shit. You gon' stand on it?"

Young Ham wasn't about to waste breath yapping. He faked like he was turning away, then spun back with a clean two-piece that dropped Talk-a-lot. The room lit up with noise.

Talk-a-lot wiped blood from his lip, licked his wounds, and gathered himself. He nodded his head, silently complimenting Young Ham on the punches. They squared off in the center of a body-formed ring, concealed from the staff's eyesight.

Young Ham knew the drill. The first fight always set the tone, and he didn't come to play. Talk-a-lot faked left, then cracked Young Ham with a mean overhand right. Stars flashed across his vision, his eye swelled instantly. He shook it off, dropped back in the paint, and let his fist answer. A sharp jab, a hook to the body, and air hissed out of Talk-a-lot like a popped tire.

The scrap drew a tight circle of boys, everyone hyped, no staff nowhere in sight. Fists flew, pride on the line. Young Ham dug in, feeding punches steadily until staff whistles cut the air. The fight broke apart in a rush.

Breathing heavy, Young Ham stood tall, his shiner throbbing but his pride intact. He had to admit, Talk-a-lot done more than talked—he backed it as well. He learned later, no matter what, everyone got tried on their first day.

Later that day, Young Ham ran into Seven at lunch. Both of them carried fresh bruises.

"You good?" Young Ham asked, sliding onto the bench.

"Like a mothafucka," Seven said, grinning through a swollen lip.

"How much time you sittin' on?"

"I got a twenty. Caught a body. These hoes gon' certify me when I turn sixteen," he said it like it was nothing, almost bragging.

Before Young Ham could answer, a guard's voice cut through. "Times up! Back to your assigned areas. Let's go!"

Seven stood, fist-bumped Young Ham. "I'ma catch you later. Hold it down 'til you touch down."

"You already know," Young Ham said, going his separate way. That was the last time he saw Seven free in the general population. Rumor was Seven caught another charge inside and landed him in segregation. Hard-time was his destiny, and he embraced it.

Life at State School settled into a rhythm. The Crips made sure everybody knew what that C-Life stood for. Nine out of ten boys claimed blue, and Young Ham felt it every time he walked the yard. He had a handful of run-ins, squaring-up on the floor here and there. All because East Austin wasn't neutral ground, and his presence meant flamed-up and bloody.

"Twelve months in the Texas Youth Commission. With good behavior, you could be out in nine."

What the hell was that old judge talking about? These small and big city hoodlums chuckled at the thought of being good. If she really wanted to know, good behavior got you eaten alive.

On the bright side, he signed up for GED class and knocked his diploma out in three months. The small victories mattered. That paper felt like a trophy, a reminder he wasn't wasting away completely.

Young Ham was allowed two phone calls a month, both reserved for

Mom or Maw-Maw. Pop had taught him better than to use a recorded line when phoning him; he knew the old man's feelings ran deeper than words.

Kamiko wrote to him once after he transferred. Said she missed him, wished she could send more, but her letter felt thin, almost counterfeit. Pop's words echoed in Young Ham's head: *"You can't keep a woman, if she don't want to be kept."*

With less than a month left, Young Ham maintained a low profile. He hadn't caught much static lately, even the staff treated him like a stand-up kid.

When the day finally came to walk out the front door, Young Ham's nerves hit harder than expected. Butterflies churned his stomach, his legs felt weak like noodles, as if he'd been squatting iron since sunrise.

The release process dragged on. Paper after paper, signature after signature. It felt like he was buying a house instead of stepping back into the world. After an hour of straight stalling, he stepped outside to be driven back to Travis County.

A black-on-black Chevy Tahoe swung into the lot, rims shining, grabbing Young Ham's attention. The SUV cut sharp toward the curb and slid to a stop, windows down.

"What's the deal, my nigg?" Stacks hollered.

The deputies froze in terror, caught between running or playing dead. Young Ham lifted his hands, grinning, and walked straight toward the truck. He hopped in, shutting the door behind him. Inside were all his day ones, something like a hood reunion.

"Damn, hood. Glad you home," Youngin' said from the back row, leaning forward. He tossed a rubber-banded G-stack onto Young Ham's lap.

Smiley, sitting to his right, grinned hard. He reached over, handing Young Ham a folded stack of hundreds. "A nigga missed you for real, fam."

Up front, Killa lounged in the passenger seat. "The streets ain't the same without you," he said, passing back a fat roll of welcome-home cash.

Young Ham had to move on reflexes, catching the money flying over the driver's seat. No words needed. Stacks was already wiping at his face, trying to hide tears of relief, happy that his ace was home.

"I love y'all niggas to the grave," he shouted. "I'm baaaack!"

Fifteen

Last time I checked I was the man on these streets. Young Jeezy poured out the Tahoe's speakers, bass shaking the frame while Young Ham leaned back, rocking in place. His mind wasn't on the beat though—it was on freedom. A whole year wasted, trapped behind cold walls, had only made him hungrier. If society already stamped him as a criminal-minded throw away, then they hadn't seen *nothing* yet.

The ride felt different now that he was home. Every block they passed carried weight, corners he once torched, faces he remembered. Young Ham realized he was seeing his city through two sets of eyes: the old him who used to run wild, and the new him—sharper and more aware. He thought about everything he lost, and everything he wanted back.

They cruised for about half an hour, smoking and drifting with no real destination, just letting the hood soak in. Stacks pulled up at Terry's Seafood, where Young Ham grabbed the famous fish plate, then had Stacks drop him off at Mom's.

"I'ma get at y'all later," Young Ham said, stepping out.

At Mom's, the comfort wrapped him tight, feeling like something he'd been starved for. But underneath it all, he couldn't shake the thought that the same streets welcoming him back were the ones waiting to test him.

Mom announced Pop's arrival, and soon Pop walked in, cool and collected. He settled on the couch, emotions hidden beneath a knowing grin. Every time Young Ham caught his father watching him, he could see the unspoken questions in Pop's eyes: Was he ready? Did he still have the heart for it?

"Look out, son," Pop said once Mom excused herself. "Roll with me one time."

Around 1 p.m., they entered Spicewood Springs on the northwest end and pulled in front of a house gated off by iron. At the push of a button, the gate pulled back, and in the center of the circular driveway sat Nika's Benz coupe, chrome rims glistening in the sun.

Pop caught Young Ham peeking. "First and last time you come to this house—we clear?"

Young Ham almost shook his head but caught himself. "Say no more, Pop. That's a done deal."

Inside, Nika sprawled across the sofa in boy shorts, puffing on a slow-burning hydro blunt. She disappeared to change clothes once they entered. When she came back, she grinned at Young Ham.

"Boy, you better come give me a hug with yo funny lookin' self," she said, blunt dangling between her lips.

They laughed it up until Pop returned. Then the mood shifted. Pop laid out the truth. He broke down how the game was still moving strong at the shop for those tampering on the wrong side of the law. Same spots popping, same risks taking. Then he dropped the part that hit Young Ham sideways—mentioning he was getting the wrong kind of attention and the Feds were watching close.

The big windows around them suddenly felt like cameras, and Young Ham felt a weight press down on his chest. Coming home wasn't just freedom. It was about him stepping right back into danger.

Pop handed him a burn-out phone, programmed and ready, plus a stack of five bands, commenting that Gs get gifts too.

At that moment, Young Ham discussed his expected return to the dope game. "Pop, I'm ready for the next level. Anything less is unacceptable."

A few minutes passed before Pop spoke. "Junior," he said, "I respect yo determination. But don't forget—these streets don't love nobody, you gotta be ready for all that comes with it. I'ma flood you with the work, you just prove who you say you are."

Young Ham nodded, fire sparking inside. Coming home wasn't about picking up where he left off. It was about claiming something bigger, proving he was built for more. Wrapping it up, they sat around laughing at the tales Young Ham told about his days in TYC.

$ $ $ $ $

Later that day, Young Ham stopped at Maw-Maw's. She smothered him with hugs and kisses like she never wanted to let him go. For a moment, he let himself feel like her baby again, and not the hustler he had become. She tried feeding him, but he was still full from Terry's fish plate.

Young Ham stepped out back, looked around, then pried up an old thin sheet. He used his phone as a flashlight, and scooted underneath the house and dug up his hidden treasure box. He added Pop's five to the pile of cash, reburied the box, and went back inside.

Stacks pulled up not long after, woofers rattling the block. Young Ham jumped in. "'Preciate you sliding through, homie."

"Man, we bigger than that small shit… straight up," Stacks replied.

"I know it," Young Ham looked himself over. "Bend a corner to the mall. I look like a downtown drunk."

Fifteen pounds heavier since his bid, Young Ham's old clothes choked his frame. He and Stacks hit the mall, and by the time they left, Young Ham had bags on bags.

From there, it was straight to Johnson's Barbershop on E. 12th. Old-head Mr. Brown was cutting Young Ham up and gossiping the whole way. Stacks, impatient as always, dipped out and bent a few corners to kill time. A Black & Mild later, Mr. Brown slapped the sting of aftershave on Young Ham's face, and he stepped out fresh.

Stacks waited outside by the Tahoe. As Young Ham stretched, a dark-tinted midnight blue Acura crept past. Their eyes tracked it suspiciously. When the car whipped an illegal U-turn, Stacks pulled a steel-gray Desert Eagle from under his shirt.

"Watch out, my nigga," Stacks muttered.

Young Ham felt naked, hating himself for not carrying. He swore he'd never be caught empty-handed again.

The Acura pulled alongside, and Young Ham's guard eased when it was four females filling the seats. The driver's side door popped open, and stepping out came a face he hadn't seen since school days.

"Foreal, I thought that was you," Sandy said, flashing dimples and calling him by his government—the only name she knew.

They hugged tight. She reminded him of math class, when she'd hold him down on classwork while he was too high to care. Sandy was a red-bone head-turner, thick in all the right places, and beauty undeniable. Above all, Sandy and her crew, *the Valle Girls*, weren't random pretty faces. They had a winning hustle and were cleaning up in the surrounding suburbs of Del Valle, TX.

"Girl, watch how you pulling up on a king out here," Young Ham said, "but what's on yo mind, sexy?"

She laughed, glowing under the sun, and for the first time since coming home, Young Ham felt a flicker of hope that maybe, just maybe, the streets weren't the only thing waiting on him.

They chopped it up a few more minutes, laughed about old times, and before leaving, Young Ham slipped her number into the loaner phone Pop had given him.

"I'ma call you first chance I get," he promised.

Back in the Tahoe, Young Ham leaned back and stared out the window. Coming home felt like a test he couldn't afford to lose. The weight of Pop's expectations, the temptations of the streets, all waited. But as he thought about Sandy's smile, Young Ham realized maybe he had stumbled onto something else.

Maybe he had just found his Nika.

Sixteen

Young Ham and Stacks turned a few more corners before he did an in-and-out at a low-ball electronics store, and purchased an all-purpose cellphone, then retired for the night at Maw-Maw's.

Calling Sandy crossed his mind, but he pushed it away just as quick. He didn't want her thinking he was pressed already. He wasn't the type to come off as clingy.

The silence gave him enough space to adjust his game plan. Coming home had already shown him what slipped while he was gone. Liana's spot was shut down, and the crew had lost discipline. Stacks and the rest had fumbled, moving wreckless, and letting traffic spin out of control until she got evicted.

The whole crew had started hustling sloppy — breaking trap rules, and letting fiends do as they pleased. Heat drew from the Housing Authority, and before long that was all she wrote. But that's how the game goes; nothing lasts forever.

After Apt. 1301 went under, Stacks sicced Killa onto Juicy across the way. Killa put his "dick-game" hustle down, and before long Juicy's trap was moving more weight and making more money than Liana's ever did. The fiends lined up like it was a corner store.

The next morning, Young Ham rolled out of bed and stretched. "Damn,

I ain't slept that good in a long time." The familiar smell of Maw-Maw's cooking confirmed his freedom. His stomach roared on cue.

"Morning, lovely lady," he said, kissing his grandma on the cheek.

"Sit down, baby. I'll fix your plate when the bacon ready," Maw-Maw swatted at him with a dish towel when he tried sneaking a biscuit off the stove.

Young Ham laughed, hit the shower, then dressed in his fit: black Jumpman tee, Dickie shorts, and the fresh retro Jordan XIII's he'd been saving. By the time he came back out, breakfast was laid, and he tore through it like he had been fasting.

After eating, he stretched out on the couch, phone in hand. A few calls later, he learned Lil Nate and Toya had been placed in a foster care home across town. The news cut deep. It angered him how their mom still roamed about, turning ungodly tricks, while his homie and sister sat like ducks, waiting on some stranger to claim them. That didn't sit right with him.

He locked in a plan: check on Jewel, then pull up on Lil Nate and Toya. ASAP.

He hit Sandy's line.

"Nigga, don't play," she said, picking up on half a ring. "Why you ain't call me sooner?"

Young Ham smirked. "Dang, babygirl. Good morning to you too." He knew Sandy had eyes for him back in school, but he had always been tangled up with Kamiko and never fed into Sandy's flirting.

"Foreal, I ain't about to front," she shot back. "I been feelin' you since class. Been infatuated with yo realness."

"Oh yeah? That's how you feel?"

"If I'm lyin'... I'm dyin'."

"Alright, check this out," he chuckled. "You know where my grandma stay?"

"Yeah, on Goodwin in that black-and-white house across from the school, right?"

"Yep. Come through then, since you been stalkin' anyway."

"Boy, you crazy," she giggled. "I'm on my way."

Twenty minutes later, Sandy pulled up. She looked even better than the day before. Chanel scent in the air, she moved with confidence and knew what she wanted. Young Ham skipped the small talk and snatched her close, kissing her like he had waited years.

She broke free, breathless. "Whoa, Foreal, slow down, boy."

"Dig this, Sandy. I ain't the guy you crushed on at school. I'm known as Young Ham now. But I could've sworn you said you wanted to be in my arms."

"Boy, I said on yo arm," she said, pressing closer. "But I ain't trippin' about being in yo arms either, Mr. Young Ham."

Young Ham eased the energy, led her to the porch, and let her sit on his lap. He spoke about deserving the world, moving with purpose, and building something larger than life.

"If you wanna be crowned queen and roll as my second pair of eyes, you gotta know yo position as well as mine," he told her, staring into her face. "So, what's it gon' be, Sandy? You ridin' or what?"

Sandy had made up her mind before she got out of the car. This was just her hustler's wife's initiation.

"For you, Young Ham. I'm all in with a pair of deuces, boo," she said with a sly grin. "Now break me off some of that fresh-out dick."

Seventeen

Young Ham and Sandy became inseparable. They lived on the edge and did everything two-deep. If they weren't shackled up at her mom's, they were camped out in the backroom of Maw-Maw's. Being with Sandy was like kicking it with one of the boys. She came correct, never overly sentimental or girly, but could switch it up in a heartbeat.

When Sandy laid out the hustling agenda between the Valle Girls, it didn't take much convincing. They lacked a steady connection, and the back-and-forth with different dealers and prices was killing their pockets — a straight dopeman's nightmare.

"Babe, me and my girls gon' push whatever. We tired of breaking bread with these lame niggas anyway," Sandy said. With Young Ham committed to the grind, Sandy felt it was only right to help her man answer the street's calling.

Young Ham stayed clear of the shop and the duplex on Viotha Dr. Pop had been on him heavily, scolding him about keeping his distance. Deep down, Young Ham felt the old man was running a borrowed time. He had a gut feeling he'd be Pop's successor before long.

One evening, while waiting on Pop's buzz, Young Ham and Sandy sat in her mom's driveway eating rib plates from Sam's BBQ. Young Ham wiped sauce and grease from his hands when his phone vibrated.

"Yo."

"Heb-seventh-bookbag-garbage." *Click.* The line went dead.

Young Ham pulled the phone from his ear, staring at it like he'd been pranked. "What the fuck?" he muttered. The voice didn't sound anything like Pop.

"What's up, babe?" Sandy asked, catching the confused look on his face.

"I don't know. Pop on some more shit. 'Heb-seventh-badbag-garbage.'" He repeated it out loud, trying to make sense of the riddle, but it only left him fuzzier.

Sandy shook her head, teasing him. "That's why you sitting over there with a cloud above yo' head?" She poked fun until Young Ham's irritation showed, then burst out laughing.

"Excuse me, missy. But in case you forgot... we on the clock right now," Young Ham shot back.

Sandy kissed his cheek playfully. "Ahhh, Mama sorry, boo-boo."

Then she broke down the message like it was second nature. "We need to run by the H-E-B on Seventh Street and check inside one of the dumpsters for a backpack."

Being out the game for a year had him rusty, but with Sandy riding shotgun, Young Ham felt anchored. She was good with the street smarts. "That's alright, Tickle-Me-Elmo... when we get there, you hopping yo' red ass in that trash can."

Young Ham predicted federal agents could pop out any second, brandishing guns on some task-force shit. The paranoia stuck with him until they put distance between themselves and the shopping center. Only then did his heartbeat start sliding back down to normal.

Sandy kept it steady on the way to her mom's, driving the speed limit for once, both hands locked on the wheel. When they finally pulled in the driveway, Young Ham exhaled. "Sandy, it's a must we cop some new wheels like tomorrow. Riding dirty in the Acura gon' get us clipped."

"I swear, boy, you be in my head," Sandy said, killing the engine. "I was thinkin' the same thing."

"Word. Soon as the sun shine, we switching it up."

They spent the night breaking down thirty-six straight drop ounces. The cookies had been situated into four quarter-kilo bags. He and Sandy repackaged the ounces into singles. Half a kilo they split down the middle — nine ounces headed to Sandy's girls, the other nine set aside for the boys in the Bricks. Young Ham bagged his and the rest.

Before the night ended, Young Ham tucked a nine-piece under the dash of each of the broken-down Volvos parked behind Sandy's mom's house — somewhat guarded by their I'll-bark-at-anything Rottweiler.

Bright and early the next morning, Young Ham and Sandy pulled up to Big Wig's used-car lot. Rows of bleeders and corner-cutters stretched like a maze. Young Ham strolled between the autos, inspecting one after another, while Sandy hung back, arms folded. A white Dodge Intrepid seemed to wink at him, like it was whispering, *psst, yeah you... over here. I'm the one.*

Twenty-five hundred in cash shut down any talk of paperwork. Sandy signed her name on the title, and just like that, they drove off. Minutes later, they were parked at her mom's, swapping the Acura for the new ride. Young Ham drove well but preferred Sandy riding shotgun. Besides, every young king deserved a chauffeur.

The gas light blinked before they even made it across town. They slid into a Kool Korner on the northeast. Sandy, usually laid back in her Air Max and Capris, had her hair cropped short this morning, rocking a Juicy Couture one-piece that hugged every curve.

"Tell that fool we filling up and bring back something to snack on," Young Ham said, leaning against the car as Sandy strutted inside like she owned the place.

Outside, a pack of block bleeders posted up along the store window, necks snapping like owls as Sandy passed. Young Ham caught their gawks, grinned, and popped the gas cap.

Moments later, Sandy came back out with a bag tucked under her arm. One of the dudes crept beside himself and blocked her in.

"Damn, you act like you deaf, lil' mama. Too good to talk or somethin'?"

"Get yo bum ass off my face, nigga," Sandy snapped, chin tilted. "You see my nigga over there!"

Laughter and clowning erupted from the crew. Feeling played in front of his boys, homeboy shot back. "Stank ass ho! Fuck you and yo' nigga… this two-three bitch."

Young Ham eyed the confrontation at length. He re-secured the gas cap and eased the nozzle back in place, hardly upset about the out-of-line comments. When it was clear the dude wasn't budging, Young Ham stepped in between, gripping Sandy's arm.

"Bro, can you let the lady pass so we can go?"

"Weak ass nigga," the dude barked. "Burn off before you get yo feelings hurt in front of yo' bitch."

Young Ham didn't hesitate. He fired off a crisp combo of punches, each one fluid, snapping the dude's neck back and dropping him on his back pockets. Before the dust settled, Young Ham's glock was out, gleaming in his hand.

"What's happenin'? Y'all niggas want some funk?"

Silence. The four bleeders scattered like track stars, sneakers slapping the pavement, not one of them daring to look back.

Eighteen

Months later...

The Bricks and the Valle Girls were on a level the city hadn't seen before. Young Ham had positioned himself as head hustler, the one everybody funneled through, and he made sure his hands stayed clean enough to keep suspicion low. He played the back and wasn't out on the block all day.

Sundays turned into celebration days. When the count came in, it averaged eighteen grand — sometimes more if the streets were wide open. His dream of stacking a milli before twenty-one was coming to life quicker than expected. By the time he hit five hundred racks, he realized he wasn't just in the game anymore — he *was* the game.

But even though his money was straight, his mind never turned away from family. He reached out to the foster home, asking about Lil Nate and Toya once again. The receptionist kept hitting him with red tape questions like why he wanted to see them, and whether his request was legit. After battling through the riff-raff, he secured approval. A date and time were locked in for the next weekend.

The cold, stale building brought back memories of State School. The same gray walls, the same metal doors that clanged shut like they were locking away a piece of your soul. Young Ham eyed the staff, already convinced the kids here were catching the same kind of mistreatment he once survived.

Sandy stayed in the car while Young Ham walked in, lugging two thousand dollars' worth of new clothes and shoes.

Lil Nate was outside hooping when Young Ham checked in at the desk. He had made the receptionist swear not to announce his arrival. Young Ham posted up out of sight and waited for the moment. A pale-faced staff worker walked off to the rec yard, and a few minutes later, Lil Nate rounded the corner, basketball tucked under his arm.

"What's up, lil one?" Young Ham said, stepping out.

The second he spotted Young Ham, the ball hit the floor. Lil Nate broke into a full sprint. "Young Ham!" he hollered, colliding into him and nearly knocking him over.

Lil Nate had grown taller since the last time he saw him. When Young Ham pulled him back to get a better look, he caught the tears in his eyes. "What you cryin' for, lil homie? You thought I wasn't gon' come back?"

Lil Nate shook his head no.

"What I tell you 'bout that? Ain't nothing changed. Boys shake heads and shrug shoulders. Real men talk," Young Ham said, quoting Pop.

"Where you been at then?" Lil Nate asked, thinking Young Ham had left him behind like everybody else.

Young Ham looked him dead in the eyes. "Understand, young soldier. When you take matters into your own hands, you face everything comin' with it. You and yo sister like family, and I'll take it there every time behind mine."

Right then, Toya tip-toed in, blushing and acting shy. From the abuse she suffered when she was molested, Toya could forget about ever having kids.

"Girl, you better come give me a hug before I tickle you 'til you pee on yourself."

For three hours, they played, laughed, and talked like nothing else mattered. Every now and then, a blue-shirted staff member circled around being nosy. Young Ham peeped their fake smiles and brushed off a lady telling them to quiet down.

"Check these out, Lil Nate," Young Ham said, holding up a pair of multi-colored Air Force 1s.

Lil Nate beamed at the exclusive kicks and headed over. Young Ham dropped an arm over Lil Nate's shoulder, giving him a clear view of the cellphone stuffed in one shoe.

"Anytime you need me, call," he said with a wink.

When one of the workers hinted it was time, Young Ham felt his chest tighten. Every fiber in him wanted to scoop them up, load them in the car, and burn rubber without looking back. Instead, he forced a smile and hugged them tight one last time.

As they pulled away, Young Ham leaned back in the seat, staring out the window. He fought hard to hold it together, but inside he was breaking. He knew better than to let his emotions dictate his moves. But now, saving Lil Nate and Toya was part of the grind.

Nineteen

Young Ham was turning eighteen in a few weeks. Nothing spectacular stood out on the agenda. Alive and free worked well for him. But let Sandy tell it, she had other intentions and wasn't trying to hear any of his boring, old-man vibes.

By the way she cut up, you would've sworn his birthday fell on a federal holiday. Young Ham kept busy, acting like her words went in one ear and out the other, but Sandy stayed on him, determined to make it special.

"Are you listening, Young Ham?" she asked.

"Yeah, I heard you," he said, only to quiet her down.

Sandy ignored his dismissive tone. "Babe, I know you not the flashy type and don't like attention. But you only live once. Why not enjoy the fruits of yo labor?"

"Happy birthday, baby!" Mom's voice thundered through the phone early that morning, shaking him out of his sleep. He sat up, rubbing his eyes, when Sandy walked in holding a bag of breakfast tacos from Amaya's, his favorite Mexican spot.

He grubbed, then hit the shower. He was rinsing soap from his face when the door opened and closed. A moment later, a naked Sandy stepped in. Gracefully, she dropped down in front of him, looking up seductively.

"Happy birthday, King Ham," she whispered, sealing it with her own kind of gift.

Around a quarter to 9 p.m., a chauffeured Rolls-Royce Phantom ferried the couple to the Expo Center. Pop had gone over the top, renting out the venue to make sure Young Ham's birthday felt like a true takeover.

When they arrived, a neon sign blazed across the building: *King Hustler's Ball.* Not a single parking space was empty. Sandy stepped out looking lethal in a strapless Dior dress and knee-high boots. Even Young Ham had switched his thug fit for the occasion, looking GQ from head to toe.

A 2.5 carat diamond slumped off his ear, and diamonds shimmered around his customized watch — another gift Sandy had copped for her soldier.

"You killing it, daddy," she said as they headed in.

"The champ is here," he hollered at the top of his lungs.

The crowd inside erupted as they walked in, welcoming the young boss and his boss lady. A spotlight from above hit them, and the DJ cut the music.

"Here it is, party people! We all here tonight to pay tribute to the undisputed King of the Bricks, Young Ham! On the count of three, I want everybody to chant Happy Birthday to a certified hustler. One… two… three!"

Stacks, Smiley, Youngin', and Killa pushed through during the harmonious singing. Their CKC (Cash Keepers Clique) emblems swung back and forth on gold chains. The DJ flipped into Rick Ross' "Everyday I'm Hustlin'," and the whole place went wild. Sandy went one way and Young Ham went the other.

In the middle of it all, Young Ham felt a tug on his shirt. He spun around, ready to check whoever touched him, but froze. Standing there was the last person he expected — Kamiko. She was still bad to the bone, and unforgivably thicker than before.

"Why you act like you can't call nobody?" Kamiko said, acting like she deserved an award for falling short at his worst moment.

"Kamiko, miss me with all that," Young Ham shot back. "Ain't nobody tryna hear no excuses why you didn't stay down."

"Young Ham, I'm sorry. But don't forget… you left *me*."

Before Young Ham could respond, Sandy appeared at his side, wrapping an arm around his waist. "Babe, this one of yo groupies?" she asked coldly, sizing Kamiko up.

Kamiko bristled. "Excuse you. You don't know me like that."

"I don't need to," Sandy snapped. "I know yo kind. Now excuse us before you get fly and I beat that ass."

They turned to leave, but Kamiko had to throw in the last word. "Ghetto-ass."

That was it. Sandy kicked off her boots and rushed her. She swung fuck-a-bitch-up punches fast and wild, driving Kamiko backwards into the cheering crowd. The crowd parted, then swarmed back in, circling like it was a prize fight.

For a moment, Kamiko held her own, dropping her head and unleashing a load of windmill swings. But Sandy was fueled by rage. She grabbed a fistful of Kamiko's hair and yanked her down hard. With her other hand she pummeled Kamiko's face again and again, each blow drawing louder shouts from the crowd.

Young Ham had seen enough. He lifted Sandy off her feet and hauled her off. Even restrained, Sandy managed to throw one last vicious kick to Kamiko's ribs, leaving her curled up in agony.

The DJ slammed the lights on and cut the music. "Everybody out! Cops on the way!" he barked into the mic. Before shutting it down completely, he sent one final shout over the speakers:

"Happy B-day, Young Ham. The sky is the limit!"

Twenty

Shit was falling apart — and fast. Juicy's spot felt hotter than Mexico in June. The Housing Authority was sick of neighbors nagging about the same apartment and its constant traffic. The manager had had enough, filed reports with the department left and right, and soon APD was staking out Juicy's front door.

Cops were parked across the street watching every move. On some days, they sat there for hours, choking the flow of customers and drying up profits. This bothered fiends who didn't want to risk getting hemmed up, so they doped and peddled elsewhere.

By the time the smoke cleared, Juicy's money maker pumped slower than molasses, and eventually melted under the heat of the laws. Weekly profits were at an all-time low, and getting worse. Instead of fighting over scraps, Young Ham understood when crew members branched out and decided on getting money on the go. Cash keeping had become all they knew.

It only got worse. Smiley was out on house arrest, strapped with an ankle monitor. He made a bad move that landed him on street parole and a possession charge, trying to make ends meet in the back of the Salvation Army downtown.

Since the projects were too hot to touch, Stacks hit the road again, posting back up northeast. He planted himself inside Wellington apartments and went full grind. Youngin' followed his brother's lead and jumped ship too.

Killa, meanwhile, laid low on the run, ducking and dodging one-time at his best. A grand jury indicted him for aggravated assault, and a warrant hung over his head. The word spreading in the streets was that Killa. Spaghetti, and BC had bum-rushed CoCo's gambling shack, ski masks on, and laid everyone down.

But instead of clean work, one dice game participant got bold enough, and chose a bullet over breaking himself. Killa rang that boy's bell for disrespecting his gangster. That single move put Killa on the laws' radar.

$ $ $ $ $

If it wasn't one thing, it was another. Sandy had her own ways of throwing curveballs. She dodged his calls for two days straight. No text. No check in. After more than a year of riding together like yin and yang, the silence made Young Ham suspicious. When he questioned her, Sandy flipped it on him, acting like he was the one tripping and needed to chill.

Young Ham wasn't insecure, but he wasn't anybody's puppet either. If Sandy wanted to be on that new behavior vibe, he only took it as one thing — she was moving foul

Without wheels of his own, Young Ham slid alongside Youngin' in a big-body DTS, gliding down East Side alleys like they were skating on ice.

"Hold up, hold," Young Ham said, motioning Youngin' to slow down. They were in the back of a vintage '50s home. It was ghostly looking and run-down but still standing. "This gotta be it."

"You sho, dog? 'Cause this spot look deserted," Youngin' said, wondering what Young Ham had going on having him come this way.

"Yeah, I know." Young Ham got out, closed the door behind him, and told Youngin', "Thanks, homie. I'ma call you when I'm ready." Youngin' drove off, music banging through the neighborhood.

Young Ham climbed over a chain-link fence, cut across a patchy backyard, and went up a set of creaky wooden steps. At the door, he twisted the knob twice left, once right. The old lock groaned, but it gave.

"Back here," Pop called from a distance.

He joined Pop and Nika inside a dust-covered room that looked like it had been pieced together by someone's antique-collecting grandmother. A gangster-size bed swallowed most of the space, and to the left a porcelain lamp sat on top of a glass lampshade. Pop and Nika had heavy expressions on their faces like they were in the middle of a chess game.

"Man, it's hard to make a dime, let alone move a brick," Young Ham stressed. "Bitch-ass laws on a nigga nuts tight."

Pop wasn't new to the struggle; he'd seen this movie before. "Have you stopped to think maybe you outgrown yo' hustle?"

"What you mean, Pop?"

"You think you and yo' boys gon' keep winning without somebody dropping salt? Niggas hate for less. A trap got maybe three months tops. Then them people coming. Always think what's next."

He stood, motioning for Young Ham and Nika to follow him to the kitchen. Pop pulled out a Pyrex measuring cup and a bag of coke. "Son, if you lose in the game, change the rules in the game."

The room grew quiet, only the flicker of the pilot flame filled the silence. "Pay attention, 'cause I ain't cooking yo' dope no more. From now on, it's on you."

Young Ham watched close, soaking in every detail as Pop turned powder into gleaming rock. He moved in and replaced Pop at the stove and cooked up three solids of his own. After culinary arts class ended, Young Ham prepared to leave, but stopped at the door when Pop said, "Only come back here if you absolutely have to."

Later, Young Ham and Youngin' bent corners through backstreets getting toasted. His phone flashed and he looked down at the screen. It was Sandy.

"Young Ham, I'm sorry," Sandy said, slow-spoken.

"What?" Young Ham said, confused. "Sandy, what you sayin'?"

"Please forgive me, my dude just got out. We can't—"

Sandy had done enough explaining; what more was there to say? He wasn't about to listen to her fake sympathy offerings. So like Nino Brown, he "canceled that bitch."

Young Ham found out the hard way. Word spread that Sandy was 23-AL's girl, and he had just touched down from a short stint in federal custody. The streets confirmed how he gave the game a black eye... snitching on Big Hennessy and getting him a sentence only a calculator could add up. Big Hennessy hung himself in a cell after too many rats pointed fingers.

Now it clicked why Sandy, at her age, carried herself like she'd been soaking in the game for decades. Young Ham wasn't mad at the player or the game, and he damn sure wasn't bitter over a shot of temporary love. But for future reference, the next female he let get close would not have had dates with the streets.

Juicy and her overcooked rock spot in the Bricks didn't last long either. The Housing Authority cut her lease, forced her out, and just like that another hole in the hustle opened up. It took some convincing, but Young Ham talked Rodney, a used-up smoker who lived at the bottom of the hill, into renting his lease for six months.

"So you sayin' I got the layout to myself," Youngin' said, rubbing his hands greedily.

"Shit, everybody out of pocket," Young Ham said as he and Youngin' settled inside apartment 2803.

"It might take a minute to spark it like we did up the hill," Youngin' said, passing the blunt.

Young Ham hit the fruity roll-up and smiled. "Dope don't need no marketing team. It sell itself. Once word get out we got that clacker in the Bricks, fiends gon' crawl out they grave for a hit."

Rodney's old apartment turned into a new cash register overnight. By the end of the week, the living room was stripped of furniture, replaced by folding chairs and a microwave.

"That's all you think you need, my nigga?" Young Ham said.

"Shit, ain't like we throwing a bachelor party," Youngin' responded.

Young Ham bought a Toyota Camry off Craigslist, nothing flashy — just something that blended in traffic. He started bouncing from hotel to hotel, booking rooms with kitchens so he could cook in peace.

Since he mastered the art of cooking, ounce orders came in nonstop. His money line moved half a bird a day. When he insisted on paying Pop up front, Pop schooled him that all kingpins sprouted from the dirt by getting dope on consignment.

Youngin' brought it to Young Ham's attention that they were getting bird fed; unintentionally. He sold them ready-hard when buying soft was the better bargain. Young Ham requested two bricks from Pop, but under one condition: Youngin' had to go pick it up himself.

"You ain't said nothin' but a word, hood," Youngin' said as he and Young Ham fist-bumped. "Where it at… Alaska?"

Twenty-One

"**I** *done got me fifty ounces out a bird in this bitch,*" rapped Pimp C from UGK's *Ridin' Dirty* CD.

Young Ham nodded his head to Pimp C's *Murder* track, the lyrics drilling into his mind while he sat on the hotel bed counting and rubber-banding thousand-dollar stacks.

He jumped to his feet, pressed rewind on the portable stereo, and ran the same line back damn near twenty times. *What the fuck Pimp talkin' 'bout?*

Logically, a "bird" — like Pimp said — was a kilo. That was thirty-six ounces, not fifty. How the hell was Pimp C squeezing fifty out a bird? The math had Young Ham pacing the room, head pounding like he was reading the same numbers back and forth, but hitting a dead end every time.

Instead of frying his brain, his thoughts landed on the one person who could make sense of it: Keno from the Cedar Block.

Keno was cut different. Solid as they came. He had a gangster-fied rep that carried weight in the streets, known for pushing packs without breaking a sweat. If anybody could put the whip-game on a brick and stretch it, it was him.

"Fam, I need to run something by you one time," Young Ham said when Keno answered.

"Cool," Keno said. "I'm at Galloway's right now. Come see me."

"Bet."

Young Ham stuffed the counted cash into a plastic grocery sack, slid it under the mattress for safekeeping, then dipped.

Galloway's sandwich shop sat in the heart of the Eastside, between the White Swan Lounge and the infamous Sam's BBQ on 12th Street. Growing up, Uncle Bo always warned him, "Nephew, don't let me catch you on 12th Street."

But if your mouth watered for action, 12th Street was the perfect place. It was the only strip in the city alive twenty-four-seven, and today was no exception.

Young Ham pulled up in the Camry, sliding into a tight spot between two cars outside the Drive-Thru convenience store. Pipe-heads had already tore through half the lot breaking into vehicles, so parking was slim.

He wedged his way out the car and spotted Keno's Lexus ace-deuced in a slot the owner charged a fee to occupy, already hip to the area's popularity.

Inside the sandwich shop, the noise level was loud enough to make ease dropping damn near impossible. Keno and his baby mama, Poocey, held down a corner table. When Young Ham approached, Keno stood and embraced him with brotherly love.

"Big bro, you know I'ma come straight laced at all times," Young Ham said. "Ya boy tryna graduate. Teach me how to whip."

"Say no more," Keno replied, handing Young Ham a turkey and Swiss cheese sandwich. "Hit me in the morning and I got you. I see the hunger and I know it ain't for that sandwich."

Staying true to his word, Keno and Young Ham stood shoulder-to-shoulder inside the suite's small kitchenette. Keno worked the Pyrex like it was breakfast duty, showing Young Ham a new style.

Pop had his old-school stove-top method while Keno used the microwave, and worked dope-boy magic.

"You'll never learn from the sideline," Keno told him. "You gotta get your hands dirty in this game." Keno had already whipped three perfect looking zips trouble-free.

He dropped grams in the Pyrex, showered it in baking soda, then handed it to Young Ham.

"Slow up, nigga. That's good," Keno said, watching Young Ham's water-to-powder ratio.

Young Ham covered the Pyrex with a sandwich bag, slid it into the microwave, and set the timer.

Beeeep!

Steam filled the air when Young Ham cracked it open. Ether fumes ascended, forcing him to turn his head. He grabbed a fork and worked the gel in circles, wrist moving like he was whisking eggs. The dope spun in a hurricane-like motion, puffing up the more he worked at it.

"Don't overdo it, peeps," Keno warned. "Quality over quantity. Control your whip if you want the streets on lock."

When the drying phase hit, Young Ham ran the Pyrex under cold water. Just like magic, the ounce loosened and twirled its way to the top.

Now came the test. The weigh-in. Young Ham's eyes stayed locked on the digital scale, his heart thumping while the numbers rolled. It landed on 28.7.

Keno burst out laughing. "Damn, Timothy McVeigh, you blew that shit up," he said, shaking his head. "That's too much. That ain't nothing but cornbread dope right there."

He stood over Young Ham, coaching and correcting through three more rounds. The next readouts told the tale: 25.5, 26.3, and 24.8.

"Well hell, looks like my job is done," Keno said proudly.

Young Ham had nothing but love for his homie. The gratitude weighed in his chest. This was priceless game. He dapped Keno up hard, and thanked him before he left.

He dead-bolted the door and got right back to work, getting lost in the task at hand.

It was almost two in the morning when Young Ham wiped sweat from his forehead. He had fought off exhaustion more than once but kept his focus steady. With one last push, he plucked the whole chicken clean.

As he glanced over the amount of dope he had whipped up, pride hit him hard. Victorious, his chest swelled while the words off Pimp C's track rapped loud in his head —

"I done got me fifty ounces out a bird in this bitch!"

Twenty-Two

Recuperating from a long night in the kitchen, Young Ham crashed on the couch at Maw-Maw's. His kinfolk Base, Uncle Ricky's oldest son, cut his rest short with a playful jab to the jaw.

"Slippers count, kinfolk!" Base laughed, slapping fives as Young Ham got to his feet. "I know if you dozing off, it's from chasing that cheddar."

Base had caught wind of Young Ham's power moves in the streets and drove down from Elgin, TX, to see if he could catch in on the action. Out on the front porch, the conversation deepened.

"Family, I'm the street mayor of E-town," Base said, trying to convince Young Ham that he was locked to the grind. "If you funnel through me, I can tie down the surrounding town. Your work combined with my hustle… we can't lose."

"Let's do it," Young Ham replied, sending Base back up the highway with a quarter-kilo tucked inside the Grand Marquis's A/C duct.

Young Ham's next monetary move came in the form of Nika's homegirl, Lexi. She had that *I-know-I'm-the-shit* attitude and thought Young Ham had fallen victim to her slim waist and pretty face. She quickly realized he wasn't the average hustler.

Lexi had her own crib, with an attic that served as Young Ham's dope storage. What held their so-called relationship together was her good sex and fire head. She introduced Young Ham to her half-brother Ruler from Bastrop, TX. Every week, Ruler and his boys came through and scooped three zones apiece, agreeing that good product at good prices made the short trip worth it.

One night while stopping for gas, Young Ham crossed paths with Ant — a gangster type he hadn't seen in a while. Ant pulled up in a black-rimmed Dodge Magnum.

"Damn nigga, last time I seen you, you was a lil' nigga knockin' shit out. Now yo weight up," Ant said.

"That's what three hots and a cot do," Young Ham replied. "I see you ridin' clean. What you got going these days?"

Ant shrugged. "Man, I tried to cop some weight, but ended up burning gas. Niggas don't be having it like they swear they do. I'll get at you though."

They swapped numbers and promised to do business later. Ant's pops was in the Army, stationed at Fort Hood. Ant had the service city and Harker Heights in his back pocket. When they finally linked, Young Ham blessed him with nine hard for a player's price. Ant's face lit up at the easy flip.

Within ten days, Young Ham had moved fifty. Between highway licks and serving corner boys, his clientele doubled. Stacks and Youngin' were flooded with all the flour they could handle.

Young Ham thrived under the shine of brick status, as he watched the hustle come together piece by piece. Posted at Maw-Maw's one evening, he counted profits from a job well done when Stacks' panicked call threw him off.

"My nigga, turn it on the news! ASAP!"

Bills tumbled from Young Ham's lap as he fumbled for the remote. His chest tightened as the 5 o'clock news lit the screen.

Breaking... News... Breaking... News...

Cameras showed police wrecking havoc on the grounds of Rolling Thunder. Heavy law enforcement moved in, made arrests, and placed unlucky bodies into patrol cars by the threes. Reporters kept a safe distance as federal agents ripped through the scene.

One reporter's voice rose over the mayhem: a two-year investigation had finally landed. Uncle Bo was photo I.D.'d and rushed off in cuffs, painted as a major player in a smuggling ring — presumably cocaine — that stretched across counties and states.

Then the hammer dropped.

"Ladies and gentlemen, we've just been informed that the mastermind behind all the activity happening here today… is a Mr. Foreal Hamilton. At this moment, Mr. Hamilton has been apprehended and is in federal custody."

The camera shifted, and there it was — Pop, shackled up, walking stiff, his face blank as marshals stuffed him in the back of an all-black Crown Vic.

Young Ham froze. His heart sank like a stone and damn near stopped beating. Staring at the TV, he couldn't blink, couldn't move. His whole body tensed like somebody had reached inside and ripped out his life line. The truth hit: everything has an ending. But he never imagined facing it without Pop.

Twenty-Three

Tears slid down Young Ham's face but he didn't even bother wiping them. Pop wasn't just his old man, he was the blueprint, the rock, the reason Young Ham believed in himself. Every move Young Ham ever made, every risk he took, every stack he counted had Pop's voice humming in it. Pop's coaching reminded him that survival was more than luck. It was skill, discipline, and heart.

And now, just like that, the game had snatched him away.

Young Ham thought about the lessons Pop drilled into him — the codes of loyalty, the pride of never folding. He thought about the time he watched Pop cook in the kitchen as if he were a master chef. He thought about how every man in the neighborhood either respected him or envied him, but nobody had his stripes.

The thought of walking forward without Pop's hand guiding him made Young Ham's stomach twist. He felt like a kid again, abandoned, even though he was standing tall in his own grind. The tears turned to anger, then to fear, then back to grief.

He knew nothing in the world was forever. But in his mind, Pop was supposed to be untouchable — one of those men the Feds couldn't cage, the streets couldn't kill, and time couldn't touch. Seeing him shackled broke something inside Young Ham, something he didn't even know could break.

Young Ham whispered to himself, barely audible, like a prayer and a promise all at once. "I got you, Pop. Even if you ain't here, I got us."

But inside, the truth ate at him — nothing in the streets would ever feel the same again.

$ $ $ $ $

Pop had been in federal detainment for over a month. Nika wasn't even at the shop when the raid went down, but the alphabet boys still hunted her down and dragged her in as an accomplice to Pop's hefty stack of charges.

Young Ham shut himself off from the world during that time. He didn't bother going outside, and stayed locked up in his room at Mom's house. Most days he buried his head under the covers, and slept long hours. He showered only every other day, and barely ate. Nights were spent wide awake, grieving, and wondering how he'd survive without Pop's guidance.

Stacks called and tried keeping him grounded. "Damn, homie," Stacks said. "You got a nigga out here worried and shit."

"You know it ain't nothing but love. I ain't gon' lie though, that Pop shit fuckin' with me tough. Some days I wanna go on a rampage and toe-tag every nigga hatin'," Young Ham's voice crackled, getting upset all over again.

It was funny how everyone assumed he had lost his mind after Pop took that fall, or that he was soft because Pop's reputation had somehow babied him. Like he couldn't stand on his own.

"In our world, soldier," Stacks said, "real niggas get raw deals. Bump what these pussies sayin'. Get right so we can get back to that scrilla. One love, homie."

Youngin' and Smiley called to check if he was breathing. The rest of the world wanting something to gossip about faded into voicemail hell. The d-boys looking to restore stopped blowing up his money line after a series of not answering. He cut himself off completely, tossing his reachable lines and going phone-free.

Then Pop's words came back to him: *Hey, only come back here if you absolutely have to.*

Young Ham smiled at the memory. He rushed getting dressed before barging into Mom's room. "Ma, I need to run a quick errand. Can I borrow yo' car, please?"

"Foreal Junior, be careful, and make sure you bring my car back in one piece. You hear me?"

"You good, Ma, I'll be back in a minute. I love you." He snatched the keys before she could change her mind and hurried out.

Minutes later, he killed the engine in an empty cul-de-sac and crept around back. After the familiar combination of twists and turns, the old door creaked open. To his surprise, Max leaped up and licked him excitedly, tail wagging. Young Ham felt the same emotion and let Max lick his face — just for today.

He shut the door, eyed the once-ferocious Doberman, and set out dog food and water, then stood in the kitchen, remembering his first cooking lesson.

Strips of sunlight warmed the house, guiding him through the silence. Max padded along as they entered the bedroom where he had last seen Pop and Nika together and free. He shook his head, sitting on the bed. The hideout held too many ghosts. *I'm not ever coming back here.*

Max jumped onto the bed, knocking the antique lamp to the floor.

"Get down, Max," Young Ham snapped, bending to clean up the mess.

He spotted a crumpled manila envelope among the shattered porcelain. Tearing it open, bundles of cash spilled out — money stacked like it had just come off an armored truck. Wedged between the stacks was a folded sheet of paper. A letter, addressed to him.

Son, If you are reading this, then the circumstances of the lifestyle we call the 'Game' have flipped to the other side of the two-headed coin we live by. What I told you — and more importantly, what you internalized your young life will show itself when you're faced with uncertainty. Nothing in the streets is to be taken for granted. Every step and every decision must be considered major, no matter how big or small. Always know that you come from kings. So get your paper while the getting is good, and when all else fails, keep it real by keeping it street. Contact (713) 888-1111. Take the money and go alone.

The words blurred for a second as Young Ham stared at the page. His chest felt warm, like Pop had reached out from the cell and grabbed him by the collar.

This was more than advice; it was confirmation. Everything Pop had been drilling into him since he was a shorty — all the lessons in loyalty, survival, and hustle — was right there in black and white. Pop had known this day might come.

Young Ham thought about the nights Pop would sit him down, breaking down moves like a coach drawing up plays, always saying, *"The streets got rules, but first it's about survival. Never let nobody write up the ending but you."*

Now here he was, letter in hand, realizing these weren't just stories or game talk. Pop wasn't just preparing him for the hustle — he was preparing him for life without him.

Young Ham swallowed hard. Losing Pop had ripped a hole through him, leaving him drifting. But this letter? It was an anchor and a push at the same time — painful, but necessary.

Before Young Ham could stand up fully, a glimmer between the broken shards caught his eye. He reached down and picked up something metal that resembled a cigarette lighter. He turned it over and noticed the initial engraved on it, rubbing his thumb across the gold-plated *M*.

He smiled, half proud, half broken. *That's Pop,* leaving him a piece of him even in this mess.

He pocketed the lighter, the letter, and the bundles of dead presidents. Then he and Max walked out — for the last time.

Twenty-Four

Young Ham had been trapped too long in that self-pity cocoon, drowning in grief and silence. But something in him snapped—today he was done with all that and decided he'd bury the sobs and worries of yesterday by getting outside. He still hadn't contacted the number Pop left behind. Up until now, no hustling had gone down. But that was about to change.

What ate at him the most about his short break from the game were the whispers, the rumors floating that he was washed up, done. The crazy thing was, just a month ago he had towered the hottest blocks as King Hustler. But in the streets, memory was short. Now they acted like he was through.

But above the dirt throwers and the player-hating talk, he knew one thing for damn sure—he needed a serious cocaine connection. That was the only way to shut everybody up and remind the city who he was.

$ $ $ $ $

Killa was still stuck in the county, stressing under the fluorescent lights, and lost in the cycle of court resets every month. Young Ham felt that weight too. He had already dropped a bag on the table and hired a lawyer to either beat the case, or at least shave Killa's time down, something short, where his boy wasn't an old man before he touched daylight again.

The prepaid lawyer had it mapped out; if the state's key witness didn't show up, Killa walked. But if that man stepped in front of a jury and pointed fingers, convincing twelve strangers otherwise would be an uphill battle.

Those words kept circling Young Ham's mind as he rode shotgun in Stacks' black 750Li, the tint dark and the chrome Lexanis spinning clean. The leather felt cold under him, but his mind was hotter than ever.

"How it feel to be back?" Stacks asked, lowering the bang at a red light.

Young Ham stared out the window. Part of him felt like the city dared him to claim the streets again. "I don't know yet," he admitted. "I'm still lookin' at it."

"You already know what time it is," Youngin' said, leaning forward from the back. "It's time to pick up where Pop left off."

Stacks nodded. "Youngin' right. What we need is that plug yo' old man had. That's the ticket."

Young Ham shifted at the mention of Pop. The name always sparked something inside. He couldn't lie though—he missed it. The rush of fast money, the streets loving him one minute and all that came with it the next. He felt the old hunger clawing back.

"I been sittin' on this number Pop left me," Young Ham said. "I'ma see what's up in the morning. Vacation over… it's back to ballin'."

Stacks grinned and pulled the Beamer into the neighborhood strip, parking outside T-Shirt Connection, the spot where you could get your set or clique name stitched bold across a hoodie or tee.

They sat waiting while Stacks twisted "doe-doe" he copped from Pickle Street. Young Ham had sobered up during his hiatus. It made him think clearer instead of clouded. He understood why folks did it though. Some lit up to forget, others smoked to remember.

That's when Young Ham's eyes locked on a pedestrian sliding past the Beamer, headed toward the store. His heart skipped. He knew the face.

"Heads up," Young Ham said coldly. "That's the witness on Killa's case. Same dude from the profile pic."

Stacks leaned forward, squinting. His face turned hard. "I'ma sleep this fool for interruptin' my smoke session." He flicked the half-smoked Garcia Vega into the ashtray.

They all hopped out. The dude stepped out of the store in a red hoodie with "SouthSide" branded bold across the chest, like he didn't know where he was.

"Slow up and hear me, patna," Stacks barked, "'cause right now you trippin' with yoself. Them white folks can't save you out here."

Young Ham slid a tool from his waist, cocked it, and leaned on the hood of the car like it was just another day. Youngin' click-clacked a Ruger, backing the move. The Southsider froze, sweat dripping, praying the silence would pass as a peace treaty.

Young Ham let him marinate under the heat of the moment. Finally, he eased up. "That's on you if you want them problems, Curtis," he said, calling him by his birth name.

He leaned back into the Beamer, closing the door. Stacks and Youngin' followed, and they pulled off, tires biting the pavement.

In the rearview, Curtis stood there praying, hands stiff at his sides. The man looked like he had just been handed his life back.

Twenty-Five

Ring… ring… ring…

Young Ham leaned against the busted payphone booth outside Big Al's, cradling the receiver. A couple of early-morning smokers moseyed off after mistaking him for someone handing out their first hit of the day.

"Who?" a heavy-accented voice barked.

"Look, all I know is my Pop left this number for me to call. So I'm seeing what's up," Young Ham said, not knowing what else to add, only confident Pop wouldn't have steered him wrong.

"Young Ham?"

He stared at the receiver, disgusted. *Who the fuck sayin' my name over the phone like they crazy?* Name dropping over public lines had always been a no-no in the game.

"Who this?" he asked reluctantly.

The broken-English voice on the other end ignored the question.

"Call de number when ye make it to Houston." The line clicked dead before Young Ham could respond, leaving him staring at the receiver, but knowing he'd be in H-Town soon.

$ $ $ $

Doing eighty down Highway 290 in a rental Mom had borrowed on her credit card, Young Ham arrived in the city of syrup in under three hours, bumping Chamillionaire's *Ridin' Dirty* through the speakers. He pulled into a service station, hit a payphone, and rang the contact.

Houston was new ground. He'd never stepped foot in the fourth-largest city, but he'd heard the stories—slabs crawling slow and Styrofoam cups tilted high.

"I'm in yo' city," Young Ham said.

"Where ye be?" the accented voice crackled back. "Are ye alone?"

He scanned the street for landmarks. "I'm at a Shell on Martin Luther King, off the freeway. It's just me."

"Do nothing. Me come now."

By the time Young Ham grabbed a Powerade from the store and walked back to his car, a flat-black Bentley Arnage floated across the lot, smothering the scene like royalty. Pedestrians froze, eyes wide, admiring the half-million-dollar ride.

The presidential tint made it impossible seeing inside, but Young Ham felt in his body this was Pop's hook-up. His gut told him. He straightened up and power-walked over. The back door cracked open on its own.

He climbed in, shut the door, and adjusted to the dimly lit backseat. A shadowed figure sat beside him, still as stone. He didn't look over. He didn't blink.

"I am Franco, Young Ham," the man finally said, voice steady as the car pulled off. "It's me pleasure to meet de son of a man I would give me life for."

They weaved through traffic onto the 610. That's when Franco's story spilled slowly. He was a mafia-tied Colombian, brought into the States by his cousin PePe. Through PePe, he met Pop.

Before Franco subbed as Pop's regular connection, Pop moved weight from PePe until he was murdered in cold blood by his childhood friend, Juanito.

One day, an argument behind money matters escalated between PePe and Juanito. Temperatures flared and a shoving match turned into a fist brawl that ended when PePe landed a solid blow and knocked Juanito unconscious.

After waking up and being helped to his feet, Juanito acted as if he had squashed it, even hugging PePe before he left outside to his car. Still furious, he returned moments later and emptied the clip on PePe.

Prior to his death, PePe had fronted Pop a large amount that only he and God knew about. Pop not only tracked Franco down, PePe's next of kin, on the laws of making it right and paying off his debt. He also footed the bill for PePe's funeral expenses.

"Know I am truly sorry for what ye papa going through," Franco said, shifting the conversation. "Tell me, how much cocaine have ye pushed? How much ye flipped?"

Young Ham's mind flashed. He knew fronting would be foolish, but so would underselling himself.

"I done flipped two keys a few times over," he admitted.

Franco tilted his head, unimpressed. "No disrespect, me friend, but me do not conduct business in such manners. A kilo to me is peanut to elephant."

Undoubtedly, Young Ham understood his displeasure—if there was any. Moving forward, Franco's next words quickened Young Ham's heart.

"Young Ham, me believe ye have potential for greatness, me see ye papa in ye, and me want to help ye be above de rest." Franco paused, then added thoughtfully, "Me give ye ten kilos of Peruvian flake. Show me two weeks me money and go further. If no, me must move on. Bidness is bidness no matter de face."

Franco tapped his finger against the partition, and out came a gloved hand clutching a cell phone that was handed over to Young Ham. Just then, he remembered the cash he was ordered to give the mysterious men, who dared not look him in the face as he spoke.

"Oh yeah. Pop told me to give us this," Young Ham said, handing the money over to Franco, who after thumbing through the bills shook his head in amazement.

"Ye papa has paid de hundred thousand for de exchange. He be always steps ahead of de game. Truly, I am sorry for he departure."

Franco spoke in Spanish and the driver eased the Bentley back toward Young Ham's ride.

"Ye will hear from me soon."

<h1 style="text-align:center">Twenty-Six</h1>

Getting schooled by a made man lit a fire under Young Ham. Hustling was nothing new, but Franco's words reminded him that the streets were less about winning and more about survival. He couldn't wait to get back in motion and turn hard lessons into money.

"Cash Keepers back in full effect, gentlemen. We plugged in with a new connect and it's about to be on and poppin'," Young Ham bragged inside the Tahoe, chopping it up with Stacks and Youngin'.

Stacks slapped the dashboard like he couldn't hold it in. "I gots to give it to you, bruh; when you make a move… it's major."

Youngin' shook his head, still doubting. "Hold up. Let me get this straight — you telling me you got ten bricks landing in days? That fast?"

"You heard right, my nigga, but that's not all," Young Ham said. "Only the crew get action on paying thirteen-five a book. Outsiders paying sixteen-five. That's how we moving."

The brothers nodded, knowing the value of an inside price. Their solo hustles had held them down during Young Ham's brief layoff, but nothing compared to stacking bread together.

"That's real G shit," Stacks said, fired up. "Boys gon' have to bow down or move around."

"The hood wide open, fam," Youngin' added. "A few nobodies chasing cars, but ain't nothing a nine-milli can't fix. You feel me?"

"I do," Young Ham said. "We sacrificed too much to let another man eat off our grind." He locked fists with his short-handed team.

Young Ham thought back to his corporate talk with Franco — about building something that lasted. If the Cash Keepers were pushing the envelope about rising, they had to tighten up and move as one.

"Look, when this dope land, we flip it quick," Young Ham said. "One of us hold the turf, the other flood the streets."

"I'll handle the crack," Youngin' volunteered, raising his hand. "I'm already in the 'jects and can out-cook both y'all."

Stacks side-eyed his younger brother, brushing him off. "Crack'll always be king, but I don't mind pushing soft too."

"Then it's settled," Young Ham nodded.

The energy in the truck bounced between them. It felt like they were stepping into a new lane, and the lane was wide open. The moment reminded him why they called themselves the Cash Keepers, and that alone had them charged up like never before.

$ $ $ $

Some Days Later

Young Ham turned to Youngin'. "So what's good with that shorty you was talking about? She still ready to sign them papers?"

Youngin' grinned like he had been waiting for that question. "My bitch, Casandra, locked in. She gon' war behind a nigga's dirty socks."

Casandra leased a two-bedroom duplex on Sara Street. The ducked off hideaway had the right balance. It was tucked just enough that nobody paid close attention, and cops didn't post up there unless something wild happened.

Stacks lined up another lease in a quiet neighborhood where an old lady lived next door and barely came outside. The brick house had burglar bars on every window, and the landlord didn't give a damn long as the rent hit on time. It was the perfect cover-up for a property sitting on weight.

Once the rentals were stamped and ready, Young Ham sat back and thought of the soldiers he missed. "Damn, I need Killa back. And Smiley too."

Killa had a scheduled release date in less than a month. When the state's key witness wavered on testifying about the robbery, the aggravated-assault charge vanished. Killa was still sitting in the county serving two-for-one on misdemeanors, but his return was close. Smiley had a longer wait.

$ $ $ $ $

At Smith Academy, Young Ham was on his feet in the bleachers, clapping loud and hyped like he was back on the block. "Go to the rack, Nate! He can't hold you!" he hollered, his voice carrying over the roar of the gym.

Lil Nate didn't disappoint. He crossed his man, cut straight through the lane, and laid it in smooth. The crowd erupted; but nobody cheered louder than Young Ham.

Larry, Lil Nate's teammate, was right there with him, knocking down jumpers from deep. Together, they were the stars on the undefeated junior squad, running the court like it belonged to them. Scouts whispered in the stands and already had the pocketbooks open.

When the final buzzer sounded, Young Ham made his way down to them. He pulled two crisp hundred-dollar bills from his pocket and handed them over. "That's how you win," he told them. "Keep ballin'."

"Young Ham, when you coming back?" Lil Nate asked, still holding his game ball tight.

"I'll be back on yo' sister's birthday," he said. "Don't tell her though. I'ma turn that place into an amusement park."

$ $ $ $ $

Hustling felt alive again but Young Ham was restless. Franco still hadn't called and that silence had him pacing. He passed time rapping in the ear of Adiva, the Nigerian daughter of Bridgette, Maw-Maw's caretaker.

Bridgette stepped into the picture after Maw-Maw broke her ankle in a fall. Adiva took control when her mother didn't have the strength to handle Maw-Maw at her worst. Young Ham kiddie crushed on Adiva's energy but had to cut it short once his cartel-like plug finally called.

"Be at the bus station at nine. Tomorrow. Bring no one."

Young Ham sat there for a moment, the words still hanging in the air. He smiled grimly. His days of hands on were done. If Franco had people getting dirty in the game for him, so did he. And tomorrow, the real work would begin.

$ $ $ $ $

The Cash Keepers sat across from the Greyhound bus station, in a tinted whip watching everything. Young Ham scanned the area through a pair of binoculars. He rubbed a hand over his tired eyes and massaged them softly.

At nine sharp a yellow cab pulled up. The driver wore a black dress shirt and tie. He looked stiff and out of place. The man's twitching hands on the steering wheel was a dead give-away.

"That's him, dog," Young Ham assured, giving Youngin' the green light.

Youngin' hopped out and beelined across the street. Stacks and Young Ham half-suppressed chuckles watching Youngin' wander like a lost tourist. Youngin' quit the shenanigans and climbed into the backseat of the cab, ignoring the Spanish driver's nervous protests.

"No… no moving!" the man stammered.

"Drive off, ese," Youngin' said, laying a chrome .380 across his lap, that held more authority than asking politely.

Stacks crunk up and tailed the dope taxi at a safe distance. Franco needed to understand that Young Ham had the city under his watch, and any drug related pick-ups would be authorized at his team's expense, not the other way around.

Minutes later, ten kilos from the taxi's trunk were transferred over smoothly. The crew split up clean, leaving the Spanish driver unharmed at Eastland Plaza.

Before stepping away, Young Ham leaned into the cab with a modest grin. "Gracias, homie."

Twenty-Seven

After doing six months in the county, Killa was back at home. His old ways of earning a dollar and unchanged attitude had him back on the block with a vengeance. He wasted no time getting busy inside the Traffic House on Sara Street, breaking down raw product to be purchased by upper-echelon dealers.

Killa's security method relied heavy on a fully loaded Mac-11. He was aimed and ready whenever a customer knocked, but you could never be too cautious. Robbers plotted around the clock and had a grimy obsession with testing your hand no matter what.

"You thinkin' too much, fam. I'm good," Killa protested when Young Ham suggested he bring in another body and gun to help cover his back. "Ain't shit happening on my watch."

Young Ham wasn't buying it. Against Killa's consent, he went with what made sense — extra manpower guarding what was theirs. The ankle monitor ruled out bringing Smiley off the bench. Young Ham's next recruit was his kinfolk Base. By no means was Base a head-buster, but he wasn't a regular civilian either, and did have street smarts under his belt.

"Base, what's jumpin', family?"

"Shid, clockin'. You know how I do."

"True. Dig this, cousin. Fall over G-ma's and holler at me one time."

"Roger that. I'll be that way in a second."

$ $ $ $ $

An hour later, Base cleared the corner in a brandy-wine-colored '01 Buick Park Avenue. He pulled in front of Maw-Maw's, rattling the windows. The sun glinted off the chrome, spider-webbed spokes stretching outward.

"I see you lookin' good, boy," Young Ham said, giving Base's slab props as he stepped off the porch.

"Yeah, I got it out the shop yesterday soon as the paint dried."

"Hey, let's go inside. We need to talk cash."

"Sound like you talkin' my language. I'm all ears."

They went inside and traded words before Base made his decision.

"No disrespect, cuzzo. But I just can't up and empty the piggy bank on my city."

Young Ham understood the loyalty that tied Base to the town that raised him; he nodded, and renegotiated the play.

"Check this, fam. I'ma support all yo' pat'nas back home with dope and prices as if it was you."

Base couldn't help but smile. "Sounds like a winner to me. Let's play ball."

$ $ $ $ $

Once word spread of the Cash Keepers drowning competition with quality product at below rate prices, the Traffic House's clientele exploded. Everybody and their mommas wanted a piece of CKC's business.

Crooked L from the M&M projects reached out through mutual contact and scored a rectangle. He later sent a good word back, satisfied, and promised to hook up again on the rebound.

Young Ham knew having Crooked L in his pocket pointed at a boss move toward ruling the East. Crooked L had regulated the drug trade across the tracks for a long time.

Lil Head Ced out The Shack sent one of his lieutenants down and bought nine soft to take back to the all-red gangland. He first wanted to test the dope's potency and see what the noise was about. Impressed, he grabbed a whole one the next day.

Young Ham's boy Keno came through and purchased one and a half, not wanting to miss out on the dopest flake flooding the streets. Though the love was shown by few, the Cash Keepers sudden rise rubbed some the wrong way. Specifically, haters like 23-AL.

"Peep this, bruh," Stacks said on the phone with Young Ham. "This circus clown 23-AL trippin' 'bout me pickin' up bread in his so-called hood. Like I give a fuck 'bout his feelings."

"That nigga ain't sayin' shit," Young Ham replied. "He been on the East eating big for a while, but so what."

Young Ham already despised 23-AL for snatching Sandy out the palm of his hand. That ranked minor compared to the fact that 23-AL acted like he shot-called the corners Young Ham viewed as his. For that reason alone, he and the Cash Keepers threw up the middle finger and laughed at 23-AL's silly attempt to throw his weight around.

$ $ $ $ $

While up on the Cedar Block, Young Ham chilled with the regulars — Keno, Spaghetti, and Iceman. They were hanging in front of Eddie's, the hood's corner store, when 23-AL's H2 Hummer rolled up and stopped.

Young Ham didn't pay the vehicle no mind and kept his conversation going, until his name was called.

"Young Ham, let me holler at you," 23-AL yelled from the street, sounding more like a command than an asking.

Young Ham clenched his jaw and stepped out, knowing this was a face-off and that it wouldn't end well for one of them.

"Spit at me, AL. What's on yo' mind?" Young Ham stood a few feet away, reading 23-AL's whole character before deciding to take it there.

"What I wanna know is who the fuck your young ass think you is?" 23-AL barked, stepping up. "You and them lil' niggas runnin' around like y'all untouchable or some shit. Don't forget, your snitch-ass old man ain't here to blanket you no more."

Before Young Ham could think twice, his Glock appeared in his hand. He used it like a hammer and slammed 23-AL's skull against the pavement, repeatedly. Each strike left an ugly gash, and three Cedar Block OGs had to pry him off of 23-AL.

23-AL's mouth got him taxed, left stretched out in the street a bloody mess. Sandy didn't even get out of the car to help her man to his feet.

<h1 style="text-align:center">Twenty-Eight</h1>

All tickets were punched in a matter of twelve days flat. Young Ham phoned Franco, half-expecting to hear a hint of contempt in his voice. To his surprise, unless Franco played possum, he seemed to be himself.

"Ye remind me of meself, wanting matters into me own hands," Franco said. "No problemo. Come and see."

The mob figure wanted Young Ham to meet him face-to-face, so once again, Young Ham gassed up and headed to Space City.

$ $ $ $ $

Sitting inside a spacious Cadillac Escalade, Franco had other plans this time — plans that didn't include riding around wasting gas. He had Young Ham follow behind his driver as they rolled through to his six-acre, fully gated estate in Sugar Land. Out front, armed men in black suits stood still.

"'Tredition held in me country, when ye bring a friend over he house for first time. Ye tell friend who ye are," Franco said as Young Ham sat in the massive living room, listening to his cocaine supplier divulge his life story.

Francisco's Story

Francisco Renteria was born in the rough port city of Buenaventura, Colombia. He grew up in poverty. His home consisted of his father, mother, and six siblings — four brothers and two sisters. Francisco was the youngest of them all.

139

Carlos Renteria, his grandfather, was a powerful man, responsible for controlling nearly sixty percent of the drug flow coming in and out of the port. He was wealthy, dangerous, and feared before being murdered by rival cartel members.

Willy, Francisco's father, wanted no part in revenge. He only prayed his family could stay out of the line of fire. He worked construction, earning a day's pay each day, but there were times when the pay didn't come, leaving hungry mouths at home unfed.

Francisco's mother, Eliza, stayed home waiting on her husband's wages. When money didn't come, she made sure her kids ate first, even if it meant she went without for days.

As Francisco grew older, he realized school cost money his family didn't have. After another winter day of going hungry, he told his mother, "Mamá, no voy a ir a la escuela. Me voy para América. Te ayudaré de allá."

His mother broke down in tears hearing her son say he was done with school. She cried harder when he said he was leaving for America. Deep down, she knew it was the last time she'd see her baby boy.

It had become almost traditional for young men to leave home early, step out from under their family's shelter, and go beyond Colombian soil for a chance at sending money back. Francisco had grown tired of seeing his mother struggle and decided he wanted more. He avoided going back home and dreamed of a better life in America.

His cousin, PePe, had left one day and never came back. Searching for better days, PePe made it to America — and thrived there. The name-brand clothes and the big house his family owned proved he was living well.

A mutual friend helped Francisco connect with his cousin over the phone. Hearing each other's voices after so long brought both joy and silence. Once the excitement faded, Francisco explained why he was

calling. PePe listened quietly, then gave him a short list of instructions —
words Francisco memorized like scripture. He knew his life depended on
getting everything right the first time.

Many had died trying to do what PePe had done. Some were caught
and enslaved by human traffickers in other countries. Money played a big
role in whether you survived or not. PePe told Francisco that if he was
serious, he'd have to prove he could make it on his own before earning his
cousin's full support.

The day before Francisco set out for America, PePe warned him not to
stay in any one spot for more than a day or two. "Keep moving," he told
him. "And all you need to pack for the road is your heart."

Francisco made it to Panama with ease. Migrants were always on the
move, and most people he met along the way helped him out, offering food
or a place to stay for the night. Secretly, they all rooted for him to make it.

After a while, Francisco reached Costa Rica and called PePe to tell him
where he was. PePe wired him two hundred dollars and said bluntly,
"Cousin, this is where I'll find out where your heart's at. Don't call me again
until you're in Mexico." Then he hung up.

Francisco felt lonely — like the last soul left in the world — but he
didn't let self-pity stop him. He pushed forward, moving through
Nicaragua, Honduras, Guatemala, and finally reaching Orizaba, Veracruz,
Mexico.

At last, he made it to the port, but he knew the journey wasn't over. He
noticed a crowd of people gathered around one man speaking in the middle.
Though the speaker wasn't of Spanish descent, he translated well enough
for Francisco to understand — this was the missing piece to his plan.

The man was what people in Francisco's country called a *Coyote*,
someone who accepted payment to smuggle illegals into the United States.

When the Coyote asked if anyone had family across the border, Francisco raised his hand. The man handed him a cell phone and he contacted PePe.

PePe answered right away. Hearing his cousin's voice made Francisco break down crying before passing the phone back to his guide. After a short conversation, Mr. Coyote gave Francisco a thumbs up. Within a few hours, eight or nine people in the group confirmed they had U.S. family members waiting to wire transfer $1,500 — six of them already had American cash in hand.

The group was led to a designated location where they camped until nightfall. Then began a two-day hike through brush and scrub, dodging border patrols. Before they set out, Mr. Coyote warned them — if you couldn't keep up, you'd be left behind. No exceptions.

Thankfully, they all made it safely to the pickup zone where a van was waiting to take them the rest of the way — en route to America.

Twenty-Nine

A Hustle Later....

Young Ham flossed through the city streets in a paper-plated Maserati Quattroporte, driving like he owned the block. His ten-thousand-dollar TIS rims had boys shooting ugly looks and feeling small — but damn them. He meant to flaunt every bit of it, a reminder of what the struggle couldn't break.

He pumped the brakes at the stoplight on 12th and Chicon, his gaze locking on a sight he hadn't seen since he was younger. Lil Nate and Toya's mom, Jewel, leaned against the cracked bricks of the White Swan Lounge, copping dope from one of the block runners. She popped the rocks in her mouth and vanished down the alley.

He mashed the gas, ran the red light, then hooked a hard left. He popped the trunk from inside, jumped out, and soaked a cotton face towel in chloroform.

Moments later, he jogged across the street and cut through the back alley. Jewel was squatting behind a tree surrounded by trash and beer cans, desperately pulling the last hit from her straight shooter. Her final puff turned out to be just that — the last. The chloroform-soaked towel covered her mouth and nose, and within seconds she was out cold.

Young Ham lifted her frail body over his shoulder and carried her back to the car.

He smiled to himself, and pictured Jewel's reaction when she woke up and realized she'd been admitted to Second Chance — a rehab center with strict rules. Once admitted, patients were considered property of the institution until they were clean. No exceptions, no early outs.

He knew she'd hate him for it, but he also knew it was the only way she'd live long enough for Toya and Lil Nate to ever see her clean again.

$ $ $ $ $

Toya's birthday party had Young Ham drained. He'd dropped nearly five grand turning the once gloomy foster home into a place of joy — balloons, pizza, and laughter echoing through the halls. The kids ran wild, giggled, and chased each other for hours.

Young Ham brought Max along. He tired himself out barking and scaring the kids. Max settled down enough for Toya and him to snap selfies. Toward the end of the day, Lil Nate clung to Young Ham, not wanting him to leave.

"Why you don't just stay with us, Young Ham?" Lil Nate asked, eyes glossy at the thought of losing him again.

Young Ham felt that. He saw the pain in the boy's face and Toya's trembling lip. He wished he could scoop them both up and drive far away from it all.

"Lil homie, if I could, I would," he said, his voice soft but steady. "But it don't work like that. Trust me, you and yo sister gon' be up outta here sooner than later. And I ain't talkin' back to the projects either."

He hugged them tight, dapping Lil Nate's back as the boy's tears hit his shoulder. His young homie wanted nothing more than to be just like him.

$ $ $ $ $

Before contacting Franco and reordering, Young Ham cut in Stacks and

Youngin'. Together they scored their biggest bundle yet. Fifty. Killa's paper hadn't reached re-up status, but he'd been saving and looking forward to going even bigger next time.

Adiva wasn't just a late-night creep. She and her two Nigerian homegirls shared an apartment on the south side, all of them junior college students. They respected the money moves Young Ham made and liked his energy. Before long, they were running plays with him too.

"You deserve the world, Young Ham," Adiva told him. "Long as I'm in it, I want to serve you and make you happy. Plus, me and my girls tryna work off some of these student loans."

The Nigerian Trio helped move sizable amounts of pure raw around town undetected. One day, Adiva dropped off an order to Crooked L, disguising herself as a pizza delivery girl — dope tucked in pizza boxes in broad daylight.

"Here's your order, sir," she said with a grin, knocking at the door like it was nothing.

By then, Youngin' was moving half a chicken a day out of two complexes in the hood. He had his cousin Big Zeke running one of the drug stores up the hill, keeping the projects flowing.

"Don't forget," Young Ham warned, "shit happens when a nigga cappin'."

Young Ham had given up debating with Youngin' about parking his Porsche Panamera in the hood.

When Smiley got released from house arrest and that ankle monitor came off, he attacked the grind harder than ever.

"What's the long face for, bruh?" Young Ham asked. "That ain't you."

"A nigga fucked up right now, hood," Smiley sighed. "My daddy hella sick and old as hell. Child services talkin' 'bout placing me in a boys' home if he pass and nobody claim me."

A week later, Old Man Dean did pass. Smiley's aunt and uncle agreed to take him in, driving up from Hattiesburg, Mississippi.

After a couple weeks down south, Smiley learned about his older cousin's Gangster Disciple ties. He rode with them to the annual Black-and-Blue Picnic, a legendary event hosted by the G-Queens and GDs from across the nation.

While kickin' it, Smiley learned the hustle game and realized prices almost doubled between states. That sparked a plan. He called Young Ham from a payphone.

"Damn I miss you niggas," he said. "Throw a dog a bone when you see me."

"Ten-four," Young Ham replied.

The following week, Smiley drove back home with a female companion behind the wheel, cuffed a "get-on-his-feet" package from the Traffic House, and turned right back around.

Without losing sleep or breaking a sweat, Stacks was pumping an average of four books a week. He supplied the Gamine Girls, Valle Girls, and was feeding the northeast, 23 and 24, out of the palm of his hand. He draped himself in designer clothes, and customized his grill with diamonds and gold.

Franco noticed the Cash Keepers' explosive come-up. He offered to front Young Ham 100 kilos and quoted something Pop once said: *All kingpins sprout to different tax brackets when they start getting dope on consignment.*

Young Ham hesitated for a split second. Franco read it in his face and smiled.

"Young Ham," he said in his thick accent, "me know ye businessman in me likey ye style. For ye, ye getting one hundred kilos in one month gone. Ye pay seven thousand a kilo."

"You saying you 'bout to front me a hundred of them thangs? And if I make 'em disappear in a month, the ticket drop to seven racks?" Young Ham asked, locking in on the math.

He repeated the offer just to be sure, then nodded. Franco grinned, sealing it with a firm handshake.

Young Ham couldn't help but think: *That's an easy three hundred thousand on my end... Hell yeah, I'm with it.*

Thirty

Pop swallowed a harsh sentence of 300 months for cocaine distribution, conspiracy, money laundering, and the dreaded RICO Act. The Feds shipped him off to the holding facility in Leavenworth, Kansas. Young Ham and Uncle Ricky — the only brother who dodged a conspiracy bullet — made the trip to visit.

They drove two days straight and stopped once to rest in a small-town motel before pulling up outside the prison gates. The massive structure rose like a cathedral, its stone walls guarded by armed officers patrolling from the towers above.

About half an hour later, gun-toting COs ordered them to empty their pockets and patted them down. Another pair of guards in blue coveralls escorted them to their assigned tables inside the visiting area.

A tense moment passed before Pop appeared, accompanied by two serious-faced officers, one on each side. Soon as he spotted Young Ham and Uncle Ricky, a wide smile broke across his face. He dismissed the COs and moved over.

"So what's new, son?" Pop asked.

Once seated, Pop wasted no time digging into Young Ham's world, his crew, his moves, and where his money was coming from.

"I been working doubles," Young Ham said. "Trying to keep my head straight. Plus, I started volunteering at the rec center. Got everybody ballin'."

Pop nodded. Years behind bars had sharpened his instinct. He could hear the game behind the words.

"Son, keep your friends and enemies close," Pop warned. "Don't ever think yo own kind won't walk in yo shoes if given the chance. When money and power mix, even good friends start seeing you as a dollar sign.

Their visit lasted two hours but felt like thirty minutes. When the COs returned, Pop gave one last nod before being led back to the place he now called *home*.

$ $ $ $ $

Barely making it back from Kansas, Young Ham got hit with more bad news — Maw-Maw had been hospitalized. Her caretaker, Bridgette, had called 911 after finding her unresponsive and struggling to breathe. Paramedics rushed her to St. David's Medical Center for tests and evaluation.

Feeling like he couldn't catch a break, Young Ham dropped everything and stayed at her bedside. Weeks passed, and despite his prayers, Maw-Maw's body gave out. At eighty-six, she passed from natural causes. At least three hundred people came to pay their respects.

Months Later

Pop's urgent message echoed in Young Ham's mind: *Handle the property taxes, or the county gon' snatch the house.*

Driving down I-35, he spotted a billboard near the Oltorf exit that read: *"Need your home or property assessed and sold? Call (512) 833-0121."*

He repeated the number out loud, exited the freeway, and loaded it into his phone.

Later that day, Adiva was in the kitchen, her hair tied back as she finished one of her mama's native dishes. Young Ham walked in and dropped on the couch.

"Hey, king,"Adiva said, fixing him a plate. "You look stressed."

"And hungry," he said, thumbing through his phone. "I gotta handle something before I lose my granny house."

He dialed the number from the billboard. "Make Way Real Estate Properties," a woman's voice answered. "This is Monique Thorton. How can I help you?"

Her tone was warm and confident, putting him at ease immediately. They went through questions and paperwork over the phone, and by the end of the call, she scheduled a meeting for two days later at three o'clock.

Adiva placed a plate in front of him and smiled. "You look stressed coming in, baby."

"Yeah, I just got a lot on my plate."

When he was done eating, Adiva unclipped his diamond chain and set it beside the empty plate. She called in her Nigerian homegirls, Kenya and Queen, who appeared wearing matching lingerie.

"Young Ham, for the king you are," Kenya said, "we'd like to royally show our appreciation."

The three women undressed and pleased him in every way.

$ $ $ $ $

Monique Thorton's office sat inside the Capitol Plaza Shopping Center, tucked between department stores and food spots. Young Ham circled the lot twice before spotting a tinted window labeled *Make Way Real Estate Properties*.

Once he parked, he stepped into the little waiting area, gave his name to the receptionist, and sat down. Moments later, a chocolate-skinned woman rounded the corner and extended her hand.

"Hey, you must be Mr. Hamilton," she said, a little flustered. "Sorry for not getting your name sooner — I'm still new here."

"You good," Young Ham replied. "I'm Foreal Hamilton."

"Alright, Mr. Hamilton," she said, laughing. "Let's get started."

As he followed her to the back office, Young Ham couldn't help but notice how her plaid skirt hugged her curves. He caught himself staring, then forced his focus back on business.

"Mr. Hamilton," Monique said, scanning the papers he'd brought in from Uncle Ricky's house, "I'll need to investigate these matters further, mainly the delinquent taxes and penalties. Once that's done, I can assess the property's value."

"It's still early," Young Ham said. "We can swing by and take a look if you want, maybe grab a bite after, my treat."

She chuckled. "I am a bit hungry, but how about lunch on *me* instead?"

Young Ham raised both hands in surrender. "Say less."

They stepped into the warm daylight and drove off in her white Beamer. After checking the house, they grabbed a booth at a popular eatery. Both ordered fish, macaroni and cheese, and a slice of strawberry cheesecake.

Monique opened up about her life as they ate. She was nineteen, in college and studying criminal justice. She seemed genuinely interested in helping him out.

"So, Mr. Hamilton," she asked, "where's your girlfriend today?"

He laughed lightly. "She called me one day and said she had another man. Guess my services weren't needed no more."

Monique giggled. "Boy, I'm sorry, but she was wrong for that."

"Yeah," he said, thinking back, "her loss, not mine."

"Hmm," she said with a smile. "I know that's right."

Maw-Maw's house sold for $220,000. Young Ham had Monique open a bank account under his name and deposit the funds. They started spending more time together, eating at five-star restaurants instead of fast-food joints.

They even hit All-Star Weekend in New Orleans, and sat courtside for the dunk contest. Young Ham enjoyed her their chemistry, and they connected like magnets. But soon, his street life started creeping in. He knew his world would stain her innocence.

To protect her, he pulled back. His underworld ties were spiraling out of control… and fast.

Thirty-One

Task Force hit Stacks and his girl with an early-morning raid, snatching them out of bed to the sound of a battering ram busting down the door. Heavy armed officers in full riot gear stormed the house, cuffed the sleeping couple and threw them into separate squad cars. Then they ripped the place from top to bottom, uncovering 22 crack ounces, 840 grams of powdered cocaine, and $478,000 in drug money.

It felt like somebody sucker-punched Young Ham and knocked the wind out of him. Knowing Stacks was now in federal custody changed everything. The game had already flipped and took out Pop. Now one of Young Ham's closest had to roll the dice on the time he faced. From there, shit only got uglier as it continued rolling downhill.

The following week, Keno and his baby mama had a standoff and shot it out with the law after an undercover's peaceful attempt at serving a warrant for Keno went left. The televised hold-out lasted eight hours until flash bombs smoked out the uncooperative couple. Temporarily, Keno and his girl were deaf and blind from the explosions. ATF ran in and found multiple assault rifles, bulletproof vests, drugs, and other illegal contraband. Then they hit the jackpot, an underground floor safe holding over a million in cash.

Things kept going south when Young Ham was phoned out of the blue by one of the regulars he supplied.

"Yo gee," Busy said. "I don't do no gossiping or talking down, blood. But my lady recognized yo spot on the big screen, and I had to make sure you knew what was poppin' with yo peoples. It's bad, hustler."

Young Ham hung up and snatched the hotel remote. He flipped to the first news station he could find. It only took a few seconds before the Traffic House incident popped up.

"Homicide crews are still investigating and trying to figure out what took place at Ninety-Seven Thirty-Five Sara Street in East Austin. We do know detectives have determined that drugs and money were motives behind what looks to be an exchange of gunfire between multiple individuals, leaving one man dead at the scene. Back to you, Rachel."

The news lady identified Young Ham's cousin, Base, as the deceased found at the home.

"Damn, kinfolk! What the fuck happened? And where the fuck is Killa at?"

Earlier that day, Adiva helped Kenya assemble ten blocks of white under the backseat of an up-to-date Monte Carlo that Queen drove to the Traffic House and dropped off. It was too premature to tell right now, but somebody must have laid in the cut and done their homework on the re-up window, because the heat jumped off not long after.

"We need to lay low 'til all the heat blow over," Young Ham said, meeting up with Youngin' at an unfamiliar locale on the westside, where Cassandra and her district attorney daddy lived.

"Tsk," Youngin' said. "Niggas be hotter than summer heat already. This come with the territory — the good and bad. Crackers already trying to hang big bro. Fuck them hoes. They gon' have to lench me too."

Youngin' had left Young Ham no room to argue. He was right. If the Feds did have them dead to rights for moving X amounts of dope, pulling up and claiming to be choirboys could do no good. But for the meantime, it was best they remained separated — if Youngin' knew like Young Ham knew.

Monique called Young Ham's phone daily, but it went straight to voicemail time after time. It wasn't anything against her, and he couldn't deny the feelings even if he tried. For now though, babygirl needed to stay on her side of the world while the hands of the streets chunked curve balls his way.

$ $ $ $ $

Young Ham sat alone in the quiet, letting the storm settle just enough for his mind to catch up to what the streets had thrown at him. First Pop. Now Stacks snatched by the Feds. Keno and Poocey dragged out the house half-dead. And Base laid out on the floor of the Traffic House.

He wasn't the type to cry or fold, but the weight of his troubles hit different this time. Death was one thing. Jail was another. But when both knocked back-to-back, you started to feel like the whole world was shrinking.

His heart told him to go scoop up his people, bring everybody under one roof, and ride this thing out the same way they came in — together. But his head wouldn't cosign that plan. Not now. Not with Task Force kicking in doors, and the news telling the whole city about the Traffic House.

Monique kept calling, but Young Ham refused to drag her into this warzone. Anyone connected to him could get swallowed up by the same darkness hunting him.

He didn't know who set off the dominoes, but he knew the ending wasn't going to be pretty. If Pop could fall, if Stacks could fall, if Base could fall — then Young Ham damn sure wasn't untouchable.

157

And for the first time since he stepped into the dope game, Young Ham felt something creeping up his spine he'd never admit out loud: this was the beginning of the end.

Thirty-Two

A week had passed and still no sign of Killa. Talk on the streets lessened, and cops had given up on piecing together evidence and trying to find leads to suspects. Killa had the right intentions of keeping his face off the scene and playing it by ear.

Young Ham camped out at Adiva's for the most part and stayed out the way, waiting to hear from Killa any day now. His phone trembled and woke him from power-napping on the couch. An unknown number showed on the screen, and he answered, masking his voice.

"Que?"

"Fuck is this?" Killa snapped. "Where my nigga at?"

"Yo, chill," Young Ham said coming correct. "This me, hood."

"Ah, shit. Why you playin', bro?"

"You know a nigga don't answer crazy numbers. I just was hoping it was you."

"My fault, but say we need to chop it up on the real. I got the word on the niggas that ran in the spizot. I'm ready—"

"Pump the brakes, homey," Young Ham said cutting in. "Just tell me where to be and I'm comin'."

"A'ight, bet. Dip through Lil Mexico when the sun tuck."

Killa referred to the predominately Mexican and Hispanic filled

Charmer's Courts projects close to downtown. He messed around with a half-breed girl, who had recently become pregnant with their first child.

"Alright, peoples. Stay put… I'm on my way."

Young Ham chilled on Adiva's couch the rest of the evening. He needed a breather. A thousand and one questions boggled his mind, but nothing made sense. He was on the verge of breaking sobriety and smoking one, but also wanted a clear head to think. At times like this, he admired Adiva most for backing up and providing space.

When the sun settled, he called out and gave Adiva the heads up before bouncing. He stopped and faced her at the door as she stood there looking worried and wanting to say something, but couldn't find the words to match her thoughts.

"Hey, don't stress 'bout nothing you can't change," Young Ham told her. "In the game I play, rules are meant to be broken. The streets love none, so if I fall flat… then bury me a G." He turned and walked out.

$ $ $ $ $

He entered Little Mexico at around 7:40 p.m., and eased the ride over speed bumps the size of boulders, venturing deeper into the projects. He picked a random parking spot and hopped out. Children played in the middle of the street, under the blinking light post ahead.

He tucked a banger down the front of his shorts before heading around back. Killa's apartment door was cracked far enough to see inside. The television played and glowed against the darkness. Killa appeared in the doorway before Young Ham could announce himself, wearing a black hood draped over his braided hair.

"Shit crazy, my nigg," Killa said to Young Ham on his way in.

They entered the living room and paused in front of a floor-model big screen blocking the window. A glass coffee table sat in the center of the room between couches on the right and left, against each wall. Killa posted his back to the television and faced Young Ham. He began explaining the robbery play-for-play.

"Bitch-ass niggas rushed in busting that iron," Killa said. "That nigga Base caught pussy and ran but they had me fucked up. I got hit in the arm but kept blasting, homey."

Young Ham wanted to believe Killa badly, and see it another way, but the bullshit Killa kicked smelled worse than it sounded.

"I swear I know them fools," Killa continued. "I bet it was them niggas be fuckin' with the two-three AL."

During the time Killa hid his face from the public, focusing on keeping his name out the laws' mouth and staying free. A full rundown on who ransacked the Traffic House fell into the lap of Young Ham.

One of the known hitters was Wild Bill, a trigger-happy gunner the streets feared because of his murder-for-hire reputation. A Bounty Hunter Blood from San Antonio named Slim, who was related to Killa through marriage, tagged along.

"Where did we go wrong, homeboy?" Young Ham said sadly. "Haven't I shown all my niggas love?"

Killa backed up a step and uncovered his head. "What you gettin' at?" he said. "I just told you I know who the niggas were. Why the fuck we standing here playin' merry-go-round?"

Instead of going back and forth on some nonsense, Young Ham blurted out, "These niggas you talkin' 'bout is Wild Bill and yo kinfolk Slim."

After Young Ham exposed the robbers that clipped the Traffic House for $75,000 and ten bricks, and murdered his kinfolk in cold blood. Killa made his move and went for the gat he kept near, but Young Ham had survival plans of his own and reached for his steel as well.

They drew their guns neck and neck, and it was a toss-up on who fired first. Both pistols erupted, sounding like thunder. Killa took a shot high in the chest. The close impact slammed him into the television set with enough force to crack the screen. Young Ham caught a hot one in the neck, and did a half-twist before crashing through the glass coffee table, landing flat on his back.

The critical shot had almost taken him out, but Young Ham still breathed and managed climbing to his feet. Killa, on the other hand, wasn't as lucky. He sat propped against the television awkwardly, with his chin on his chest; dead.

Young Ham held a firm hand over the gunshot wound and shuffled toward the door. Before leaving, he looked over his shoulders at one of the originals he had come up with, and said a silent prayer: *I'm sorry, Brick.*

He stumbled out the door walking like he was drunk. He made it to the car on his own. and planned on driving to the hospital himself. Blood soaked through his shirt, warm and sticky, and every heartbeat felt like pressure leaking from a busted pipe.

He cranked the engine, but his hands shook on the wheel. *Stay up... just stay up...* he told himself.

The streetlights blurred as he pulled out and colors smeared together. His vision doubled. His eyelids felt heavy enough to drop shut on their own.

He tried to straighten up, tried to focus on the road, but the steering wheel felt like it weighed a thousand pounds. The car drifted across the lane, bumping the curb. He fought for the wheel but his arms wouldn't answer. His head dropped, and everything went dark.

The car slammed into a parked ride head-on, and Young Ham's body snapped forward over the wheel. He didn't feel the impact, because he was already gone into the black.

<h1 style="text-align:center">Thirty-Three</h1>

Three Days Later

Young Ham lay in a hospital bed breathing through a ventilator. He had slipped into a coma after life-threatening blood loss sent his body into shock. Paramedics had done all they could; it rested on God now.

Real estate agent Monique Thorton sat at Young Ham's bedside, eyes puffy and red from crying.

"Boy, don't be trying to leave me and we just met," she said, hoping and praying he heard her encouraging words.

Somehow, Young Ham was drowning in darkness and sinking to the ocean's floor. He flapped and fought to swim his way to the top, following the sound of a familiar voice he recognized.

"Foreal, if you can hear me… I'm sorry to be the one to tell you, but I know you're stronger than the hurdles placed in your path," she paused, wiping her eyes. "Baby, your mother passed away two days ago."

Young Ham stopped swimming and sank once again. Had he heard correctly?

At that moment, the door inside the hospital room opened, and in barged two heavy-footed officers carrying one thing on their minds.

"Um, excuse y'all," Monique said, standing up and halting their emergence.

"We're sorry, ma'am," a Latino officer said, "but if you let us do our jobs… we'll be out of your way in a second."

"Y'all could've picked another time instead of busting in and harassing a man in a coma." Monique rolled her eyes and let the cops pass. "Fucking ridiculous."

"Mr. Foreal Hamilton Junior, you're under arrest for the murder of Korrell Wooley."

After the Latino cop read Young Ham his Miranda rights, his partner pulled out his cuffs and latched the cold steel around Young Ham's wrist. He secured the other end to the bedrail, assuring that when Young Ham became well enough—if he even made it to cross that bridge—he'd be handed over to APD authorities.

The officers excused themselves and closed the door behind them. The ocean swallowed Young Ham again, darker this time. His arms felt heavier and his body sunk faster than before. He just wanted to drift and let it all be over, but something inside of him sparked.

He thought about Pop, Maw-Maw, the Bricks, the Cash Keepers, the respect, the grind… and then Mom. The warmth of her voice. The way she laughed. The way she believed in him even when he didn't deserve it.

Gone.

It hurt worse than the bullet, the blood loss, and the cuffs locked around his wrist. A million memories rushed through him, each one pulling him deeper until he didn't know if he was drowning in water or in his own guilt. As he sank further, he thought back on what brought him to this point…

Growing up in the 90's, you had kids that wanted to be like Mike. Y'all remember the "If I could be like Mike" commercials. Well, fuck Mike! I wanted to be like Pop, a full-blooded hustler in every aspect.

I'd inherited a hustler's spirit from Pop, and had ingrained the knowledge of the streets inside the womb. I didn't need fake-ass Ms. Cleo reading my palms to know and understand that destiny would have it no other way than for a young hustler to sit atop the throne.

On my way to the top, I proved that the treacherous streets would render all I felt was rightfully mine; the keys to the city... and some. By first taking over and reigning the Booker T. Washington terraces, better known as the Bricks.

From block to block, I then navigated the drug-infested sections of East Austin, stacking major paper and punishing all adversaries that wanted problems with me or my crew, Cash Keepers.

From the money, power, and respect. Down to the many dime pieces I banged between the sheets. What else can I say? The game had been good to me. Here I was a hood millionaire at the age of eighteen, living a fast-money lifestyle, and respected on the streets as the undisputed King of the Bricks.

Though try not to get it twisted because this hood legacy stuff came at an expensive price, my life. So, the question remains. Was it worth it? Hmm... hell yeah! Fucking right it was. I'ma Cash Keeper till the death of me.

Epilogue

Nine Months Later

Young Ham was seated in the courtroom awaiting his fate. Ever since he had come out of the coma and been medically cleared from the hospital. He had been out on bond with an electric tracker latched around his ankle, coming back and forth to court each month. It was a hassle wearing the court ordered device, but sure as hell beat bench warming in the county.

He glanced over his shoulder and the guilt hit him hard, knowing he was the reason behind Monique's worried look. The jury had been deliberating for an hour already, and he even started to wrestle with butterflies in the stomach. Patrick Oliver, one of the state's leading defense attorneys, leaned toward his client and whispered, "I got them, tiger. Don't let them see you sweat."

Young Ham cut a bold eye at the cocky, high paid lawyer. Easy for him to say. It wasn't him on trial awaiting judgment by a box of twelve. He swiveled in his seat, and rubbed a hand over the scar that reminded him why he was here in the first place.

Having to serve one of his own with the cold steel, still weighed heavy on his chest, and probably would forever. Young Ham stuck to the g-code and handled business like a true friend. He moved Killa's baby mama out of the projects and paid for all of Killa's funeral arrangements. He also opened an account in baby Killa's name that he'd collect when he turned twenty-one.

Young Ham raised his head and straightened when the jury filed in and retook their seats. The judge adjusted her robe and banged the gavel.

The Court: Let the record reflect the jury is now seated. All parties are present, including Mr. Hamilton. Speaking through your foreman, have you reached a verdict?

The Foreman: We have, your Honor.

The Court: Would you please hand it over to the bailiff for the court's inspection? And this is the unanimous verdict of the jury?

The Foreman: It is, your Honor.

The Court: Okay. Mr. Hamilton, would you please stand. We the jury find the defendant, Foreal Hamilton Jr.…. *not guilty.*

To be continued...

Cash Keepers 2

Coming Soon!

Acknowledgements

I want to acknowledge the people who supported me through the long nights, the setbacks, and the moments where quitting felt easier than finishing. A mountain of gratitude goes to the ones who listened, believed, and understood rather than condemned. Respect to everyone who helped shape this journey, knowingly or not. This is only the beginning. For all my soldiers fighting the struggle behind the gates, keep on pushing and getting better with time. All you urban-heads be on the lookout for more street-motivated titles to come. Platform Bookhouse Publishing heating up y'all. So until then…Chill. Be Still. Read On.

About The Author

D'Shon Major is an urban fiction author who writes "dope-tales" drawn from real experiences, and unseen consequences of the street-rooted grind called the GAME. He is currently incarcerated but unapologetically in pursuance of something greater than his circumstances. Cash Keepers is a reflection of lived moments, hard lessons, and the reality behind the hustle.